Emily Steele Elliott

Father's Coming Home

Emily Steele Elliott

Father's Coming Home

ISBN/EAN: 9783337073275

Printed in Europe, USA, Canada, Australia, Japan

Cover: Foto ©Andreas Hilbeck / pixelio.de

More available books at **www.hansebooks.com**

FATHER'S COME!

"'Maggie, child, what's the matter?' inquired her mother. Maggie did not reply, for a shadow had fallen across the threshold."—Page 194

FATHER'S COMING HOME:

A Tale.

BY THE AUTHOR OF "VILLAGE MISSIONARIES,
"UNDER THE MICROSCOPE," Etc.

LONDON:
T. NELSON AND SONS, PATERNOSTER ROW;
EDINBURGH; AND NEW YORK.

MDCCCLXII.

Contents.

I.

The Letter.

"It's hame, and it's hame, hame fain wad I be;
An' it's hame, hame, hame, to my ain countree!"

CUNNINGHAM

I.

The Letter.

"MOTHER, mother, the postman's coming over the bridge--there *must* be a letter to-day!" cried Hugh Christie, running hastily into his mother's cottage from the garden where he had been feeding the pigeons. The announcement caused a general commotion within. Mrs. Christie raised herself hastily from the saucepan over which she was bending, with the quick answer, "Don't you be after flurrying me, lad, when maybe he's brought none for me. Why shouldn't he be going on further to the farm?" Maggie, Jamie, and even little Nannie, had, however, no sooner heard Hugh's report, than they all jumped from their seats, leaving their last mouthfuls of breakfast untouched, and, headed by their eldest brother,

ran quickly down the lane to meet the postman, and to inquire from him whether there
was not a letter for them that morning.

And while they are speeding on their
errand, I will tell you, good reader, who the
Christies are, and where they lived.

And to begin with the last-mentioned in-
formation, let me ask you to picture to yourself a small town, or perhaps, to speak more
correctly, a large village, so close to the Border,
that England and Scotland might both have
set up their claims to it.   Airie—you will
not find it on the map (our Airie, I mean)
—was about two miles from the coast, and
pleasantly situated upon a green slope, thickly
wooded and watered by the Airie brook over
which was the bridge mentioned by Hugh.
Mrs. Christie's little house was separated from
the village, from which it was about half a
mile distant, by this brook ; and there, after
school-hours, the boys delighted in swimming
their ships, and in fishing for such fish as were
to be found.   They were the children of a
soldier from whom they had been many years
eparated.   Hugh Christie, the elder, had been
an Airie lad, who had fought mimic battles

with the sword - leaves and rushes of its meadows, from the time he was four years old, until he was allowed to exchange these in his boyhood for a bow and arrows and sling; and when his widowed mother died, with whom he had dwelt in the very same house in which we have found his wife and children, he took to a real sword and gun, and enlisted in a regiment, which, about two years after, left for India. Before that, however, Mary Innes, his old school-fellow and playmate, had become Mary Christie; and she went with him to India, though it was a sore struggle to leave her twin babies, Hugh and Maggie, behind. But it would have been a still harder parting if the husband had started alone; and her good Scotch mother promised " to look after the grandbairns just as if they had been her ain Mary and Mattie back again;" and she kept her word. For six years she acted a parent's part towards them ; but then her strength failed her, and after a few months' illness, she was taken from them, grieving sorely that her Mary would never be able to tell her with her own lips how the children had prospered in her keeping. Meanwhile, Hugh

Christie got on bravely in India. Officers and comrades all had a good word for him, and only one trial clouded his path. After about six years, and when little Nannie was yet a baby, it became evident that Nannie's mother was failing in health, and the doctors said that nothing but her own native air could save her life. And then came the hardest parting of all. Oh, it was very hard to say good-bye to her husband, to stand on the ship with a baby in her arms, and a little one by her side, and to see the pathway of water which separated him from her grow wider and wider, until Hugh, and his boat, and land itself, were lost to her sight. Little Jamie cried sorely that night in the thronged cabin when no father came to kiss him before he went off to sleep; and Mary's tears fell so fast over her little Nannie, that her pillow was quite wet before sleep visited her eyelids.

They had a rough, tempestuous voyage home; but there was joy mingled with her sorrow, as she felt that she was getting nearer to her kith and kin, and above all, to her two children. And when the meeting time came, sad as it was to feel that she was three months too late to see her mother again, yet there was the delight of finding Hugh and Maggie such bonnie, bright children, and of settling down in *her* Hugh's old Airie cottage in which old Mrs. Innes had lived during her absence, to bring up his children to love him and to look forward to their father's return as the great joy which was to make their home perfectly happy.

Seven years had passed since her return from India at the time when our story opens, and Hugh and Maggie, the twin brother and sister, are nearly thirteen, and Jamie is nearly eleven years old; and it is a clear, cold day at the end of December—cold enough to make Mary Christie's hot porridge very acceptable indeed to her children. But the sight of the postman has even more attractions for them than the unfinished breakfasts. During the last few months the usual thin Indian letters, which old Duncan with his shaking hand has so punctually delivered, have intermitted, and the inmates of Airie home have sadly felt the cessation of what Maggie calls "the little rays of sunshine come all the way from India." The children, indeed, have

recovered the monthly disappointment—hiding
the possibility of bad news from their eyes
with a bright cloud of hopes, and assuring
themselves that the reason of their father's
silence may be that he is coming home, and
will suddenly arrive some day, to take them
all by surprise.   Jamie has read a story of a
sailor whom all his relatives had for more than
a year mourned as lost, and who presented himself suddenly at the door of his home as a New
Year's gift to his family ; and Jamie, who is
famous amongst his sisters and brother for
finding out reasons for everything, is sure that
his father has read this story out in India, and
has planned for them a similar surprise.

But the goodwife herself cannot look at
this long silence so cheerfully, especially as
rumours have reached her ears of insurrection
in the province in which Hugh is stationed.
She knows why it is that Mr. Malcolm, the
clergyman, paid her a long visit the other day
after news had come from India, and spoke of
preparation for trials which God may have in
store for us ; and she knows why the neighbours look so sympathizingly at her as she
passes by ; and she knows why, when the

other day she was tempted by a bright ribbon
in the village shop, and told the kind mistress
that she'd maybe soon want a gay knot for
her gown against the goodman came home,
sympathizing little Mrs. Scott turned away
all of a sudden to find a stick of candy for
Nannie, and stooped down without a word to
kiss the little maiden, who wondered to see a
tear in her eye as she bent over her. She
remembers that day very well, for on leaving
Mrs. Scott's, she went off to the house of Mr.
Malcolm, to ask if he could give her any further news from India; and then it was that
she learnt what nobody had liked to tell her
before, that a report had come of a fight in
which Hugh's regiment had been engaged far
up the country, and in which many had been
killed and many more wounded, his name
being on the list of the latter. Poor Mary's
hopes had buoyed her up till that day; but
she went home stricken down with anxiety
and suspense. The children, his children, could
not rouse her for a time from the grief which
darkened her spirit. She would never see
him more, she said—never show him how
bright and bonnie they were; and as every

fresh post came in, bringing nothing from
Hugh, little rays of hope which stole fugitively
through unauthorized crevices and loopholes
into the heart which had now steadily closed
its doors against hope, were extinguished one
by one as no fuel came to kindle them into a
flame. On the day previous to that on which
our story opens, Maggie had surprised her
mother engaged in sorting out of an old
drawer the black ribbons which had lain by
for many years. Mary's tears were falling
fast over them, and Maggie, who had entered
unperceived, stole out on tip-toe and ran up
to her room to let out the passionate sorrow
which then for the first time found its way
to her heart. She had, indeed, never known
her father; but then she had heard of him all
her life, and had looked forward, year by year,
to his return as to that which was to make
her happiness complete. Then his letters had
constantly made known all his love to his
home and children,—such letters, full of counsel
and fatherly tenderness, and of plans for all
that they would do when he returned—letters
which might have made proud the heart of
daughter to many a richer man than Hugh

Christie. And in a crowd all these cherished hopes, and plans, and memories rushed into poor Maggie's heart; and when she could cry no longer, she sat down on the bedside to think whether this sorrow could really have come to them; and then she unlocked a little drawer where all her choicest treasures had been kept, and silently took off the bright-coloured tie which bound together every letter she had ever received from that dear absent father, and left in its stead a black ribbon, which she asked sadly of her mother, who knew in a moment then that Maggie's hopes and hers had died together.

Not all. One hope remained—that everlasting hope which alone cannot die, and which shines out grandest and brightest when all others are quenched. For Mary Christie was a Christian. She was reserved to most people, and sometimes cold in her manner; but her heart was warm and true, and her love to her husband and children came second to a higher love to her heavenly Father, to whom in this hour of sorrow she told all her trial and suspense.

And now our story must be resumed where

it began.   Mary is standing by the door of
the cottage, shading her eyes from the bright
glitter of the sunlight on the snow, whilst the
four children breathlessly run down the path
to the bridge to claim the letter which old
Duncan must surely be bearing for them.

"A letter! isn't there a letter?" shouts Hugh
who is foremost; "*do* give it us quickly!"

"A letter from father!" repeated the other
three all coming up together.

"No, there isn't one," says Jamie, discon-
solately, "I see it in his face.   O Maggie,
we'll have to wait another whole month, and
what'll mother say?"   If Jamie had looked
in his sister's face he would have seen that
the red had all gone from her cheeks which
were pale and colourless, as she hardly breathed
in her intense anxiety.   Duncan, an old friend
who had known their father from his cradle,
looked as if he would gladly have avoided the
children.   But there was no doing this as
they eagerly crowded round him.

"It's a letter—an Indian letter, sure
enough," he said, "but don't you be flurrying
your mother for nothing; it's not—it mayn't be
from your father after all.   There's a news-

THE LETTER FROM INDIA.

" ' It's a letter—an Indian letter, sure enough !' he said."—Page 20.

paper too; don't you be dropping it, Maggie, and please God it's good news. I'll maybe be passing by here in a few minutes in case there's any." And so saying, Duncan, who knew Hugh Christie's handwriting as well as he knew his own, turned away towards the bridge, almost dreading to hear that the stranger hand which had directed the letter had traced words of sorrowful tidings within.

Eagerly Mrs. Christie seized the long-expected letter, and the same unknown writing made her pale and giddy. She did not speak till she had devoured every word of the contents, and even then no words would come until she heard Nannie murmur in a frightened tone of voice, "O Jamie, it's bad news, mother's crying;" and then she put her arm round the little one, and with a choking sob of intense gladness answered, "Not for sorrow, child, not for sorrow, but for great joy; O Nannie, father's coming home!"

II.

Plans and Castle-Building.

―――――

"Waves that journey to the shore,
Bearing snowy crests of foam,
Tell the glad news o'er and o'er,
That our father's coming home!"

II.

Plans and Castle-Building.

"FATHER'S coming home!" Oh, what a joyful cry echoed through the house as the words were repeated from mouth to mouth, while the children tried to believe that which for six years had seemed too good really to come to pass. Only Jamie was a little disconcerted, because instead of joining in the shout with himself and Hugh, Maggie cried, and he couldn't think "why she didn't seem gladder, it was *so* like a girl!" But Jamie, in spite of himself, became for a minute "like a girl" too, when the letter was read out by Hugh, to whom his mother committed the office for which she and his sister were hardly fit just then. It was as follows:—

"MY VERY DEAR WIFE AND CHILDREN,—

"I hope this letter will find you all in good health, as, thank God, it leaves me the same. My dear wife, I have written to you every month since we left our old station, which we did six

months ago in the hot season ; but I am afraid that some of my
letters cannot have arrived, for the reason that many of the posts
from this out-of-the-way place have failed, and a great many besides
myself make these complaints. If you have not received my letters,
I am afraid you will be very anxious because of the reports of all
the fighting up here, which will have reached you. We were
called out for this station very suddenly, and there has been very
hard work to do. The fever has cut off a great many of our comrades, and several more have been killed and wounded. But I
am thankful to be able to say that I am quite well and unhurt,
only being rather knocked up with hard work, which after all a
soldier mustn't mind who fights for his Queen and country. O
my dear wife and children, how often I have thought out here
of how much a soldier will dare for his earthly sovereign, and of
how much less we are willing to bear as the soldiers of the cross
of Christ, under whose banner we have bound ourselves to fight
manfully

"But now, I have been keeping the best news to the last. There
is a report that our regiment has been ordered home, and for
many reasons I think it is true, although it seems almost too good
to be true. I shall be able to tell you the truth before I close
this letter. If it really be so I shall be with you in about six
months from the time you receive this, but I hardly let myself
think that such great joy can be coming so soon. How often
I have wondered when I have seen my poor mates dying off so
fast, whether I should ever be in Airie church again, with my
dear wife and children, and have dreamt of the path from the
cottage over the bridge, and wondered whether I should be able
to tell my children from all the rest if I were to see them coming
out of the same school which their father went to when he was
only a lad.

"*Two days later.*—Yes, my dearest wife, it is all true, I am
coming home, and the order has come to the regiment, and we are
to go down country directly. Eight months more, and I shall be
with you again ! Tell the children that the time will seem short

to me, when once I know that every step is bringing me nearer to you and them, and that they must all be getting ready for father. I have no time for more, as the post-bags are being made up, and there is a poor fellow (some sort of a cousin, I fancy, at all events he bears the same name, and comes from my father's part) who can't write for himself, because of his being badly wounded, and who wants me to scratch a few lines to his wife. So with a hundred loves and kisses to you and the children, no more at present, my dear wife, from your affectionate husband,

" HUGH CHRISTIE.

" P.S.—Do you remember the song that you had from your Scotch mother, Mary, the same that you used to sing in our old courting days by Airie brook? Oh, how often I have thought of it out here far away, and how often I shall sing it in the ship that is to bring me home to you all,—

" ' It's hame, and it's hame, hame fain wad I be,
And it's hame, hame, hame, to my ain countree!'

" One of my comrades has directed the cover, as I have not a moment more to write."

Oh, what a flood of joy that little bit of paper had brought into the Airie home! When Hugh finished, and somehow or other he did not read nearly as distinctly or as easily as usual, his mother made him give it back and read it again for herself, and then Maggie put in a claim for it; and when the first excitement was over, and the steady-going clock, which would not share in any excitement, told as

tranquilly as usual that school-hour was past,
the children would hardly be persuaded that
even good news such as theirs did not prevent
hats and bonnets from being necessary in December, so impatient were they to spread the
story throughout the village.   Hugh, in his
haste, nearly tumbled old Duncan into the brook,
which check in his career gave time to his
brother and sisters to overtake him and to
console the startled old postman with the intelligence.

It might well have caused surprise to Mr.
Malcolm, who happened to be in the school
that morning, to see the four Christies enter
half an hour after prayers, without pausing
outside to take off hats and cloaks, and in such
tumultuous career that all proceedings were
suspended for a moment.   But when Maggie,
with a tear in her eye, came up in support of
Hugh, who was rather abashed at suddenly
discovering the clergyman's presence, with the
words, " O Mr. Malcolm, sir, father's coming
home ! " he looked so happy himself, that you
might have supposed that the returning soldier
was one of his own family ; and he stopped his
lesson to tell the good news publicly to all the

children, and to bid them rejoice with those
who now rejoiced so greatly after the long
months of anxiety which they had passed.
And then after school was over, every particular of the precious letter had to be repeated,
and even little Nannie had a select circle of
her tiny companions round her, to whom, as
she could not remember the letter, she was
giving a wonderful account of what her father
would probably bring with him, which summary at last came to include a real elephant,
some parrots, and possibly a baby tiger, caught
before it had learnt to be cruel, and which
Nannie was to train into a sort of watch-dog
which was to follow her about and do her
bidding.   While she was holding forth these
prospects to her companions, whose respect for
herself grew greater in exact proportion to the
magnificence of her descriptions, Jamie was
describing to another group his father's personal
appearance as he remembered it last.   Now,
this assertion of Jamie's that he remembers his
father, is a sore point between himself and the
rest.   He was not four years old when he left
India, and he persists in saying that he can
quite well recall the parting day, in which as-

sertion his mother has rather supported him.
He truly says that his father is tall, and has
dark hair and eyes, but this they all know
from his wife's description, and from the neighbours who remember him as he was twelve
years ago.   Jamie, however, makes great capital of this statement, and was not at all pleased
when Hugh publicly rejected any belief in his
brother's memory, since he overheard him boast-
ing to little Mattie Scott, who was rather great
in respect of his father's having real silver-
mounted spectacles, that he believed— indeed
was almost sure, that *his* father always wore
gold spectacles, the publication of which recollection has been fatal to Jamie's reputation as
an oracle respecting the hitherto unknown absent one.

There was no settling down to anything that
day.   Dinner seemed quite unnecessary—the
letter was enough, Maggie said, for dinner and
supper too.   Happy Maggie !   How pleasant
to open the treasure drawer, and to put away
the black ribbon, and to bind up the precious
parcel with the rosy coloured tie which had
been discarded !   How pleasant to nestle into
the little low bed that night when Nannie was

fast asleep, and to say to herself, " Six months more, and father'll be coming up to kiss us, as mother says he used to kiss us when we were babies."

The next day was Saturday. There was school for two hours only in the morning, and it had been promised the four children that they should take their dinners very early, and then start off together to gather mussels and cockles on the beach, and to spend the short afternoon there, whilst their mother went to the nearest town to make sundry purchases which she needed, and to tell her good news to some cousins who lived in its neighbourhood.

It was soon after twelve o'clock that the brothers and sisters set out with their baskets in their hands for the path which led through the now leafless wood, and by the side of the brook to the beach. It was a still, calm winter's afternoon, warm for the season and very sunny, and with good news in their hearts and bright sunshine without, the children speeded merrily on their way. Never had the beach looked so pleasant, and never had the calm sea reflected more clearly every sail and every ship upon its surface. They were all soon busied

in finding shells and sea-weed — Hugh and
Maggie keeping careful watch over their little
brother and sister, lest they should stray out
of sight.   Jamie and Nannie, however, after
running about wildly for some time from place
to place, and after having admired Hugh's feats
in climbing the rocks to his heart's content,
settled down to build a fortress with stones,
which the waves were in course of time to de-
molish as the tide advanced; and then Maggie
found herself standing silently side by side
with her twin brother, looking out at the wide
sea, and half unwilling to let the sound of her
voice break the stillness which seemed height-
ened rather than disturbed by the regular rise
and fall of the light billows as they broke on
the shore.

Hugh spoke first.   " Maggie," he began, " I
think we've got the same thoughts in our
hearts."

" What are you thinking of, Hugh ?" replied
his sister.

" No, tell me your thoughts first, and I'll
see if they're the same as mine."

" I was thinking," replied his sister, " that
this sea which touches here touches India too.

AT THE SEASIDE.

" It was soon after twelve o'clock that the brothers and sisters set out
with their baskets in their hands."—Page 31.

Perhaps one of these very waves will bring father home."

"I had that in my mind too," answered Hugh; "but, Maggie, there's something more you're thinking, and I think I can guess."

"There's a little bit of fear, Hugh, amongst all the joy. You see father's so good, and I'm afraid he'll find me different from what he wishes. He'll expect us to be very good, too, and, O Hugh, I'm not half what I ought to be; and perhaps—I don't like to say it, even; but perhaps he'll be very disappointed and not love me."

"But he *must* love us, Maggie, even though we're not quite good; we're his children, and he can't help it."

"Yes, but, Hugh, he may love us with a *sorrowful* love, if we're not like what he expected—not be very pleased. I wish I knew exactly what father would like me best to be."

"I thought of that when the letter came," said Hugh, throwing a pebble so skilfully, that it performed the dick, duck, and drake evolution to admiration, and thereby helped him out with his thoughts very easily; "I noticed that little bit in it, 'Tell the children that they must

3

all be getting ready for father,' and I was thinking how we were to get ready."

Jamie and Nannie had joined the elder ones, their castle in the sand having shared more speedily than they expected the fate of castles in the air and castles in the fire—of sudden demolition ; and they all four sat down together in a sheltered nook amongst the rocks, where the bright afternoon sun shone warmly in upon them, and near which, as they had often done before, they lit a fire of drift-wood with some matches that Maggie had brought with her— a fire most precious in their eyes.

" I wonder if father'll be very particular," said Jamie, resuming the subject; "every one says he's so good."

" There are two kinds of particular," replied Maggie, musingly; "there are *cross* particular people (like Mrs. M'Crie, who kept school when mistress was ill), who try to find every little fault out, and scold about it.   And then there are *kind* particular people, like—like Mr. Malcolm, who see everything that's wrong, but look kindly all the time, and try to put one right; and who are quick to see everything good too.   I should rather that father was particular, I think; it makes one look up more."

This was a long sentence for Maggie, but the good news from India had roused her quiet nature more than it had ever been roused before.

Nannie interposed when she had done. "It seems such a long time to wait," she said. "Six whole months! Why, it'll be hot summer time then! Happiness doesn't seem so great when it's such a long time off."

"I think it seems shorter to grown-up people," replied Jamie; "it seems shorter to me than to you, Nannie, and mother says it seems no time at all, now that she knows for certain father's coming."

"And father says the time will seem short to him," said Hugh, "but it seems a great way off to me, though I'm older than you, Jamie. I wish there was some way of making it go quicker."

"Don't you think that if we were all to set to work to do something for father before he comes, the time would seem much shorter?" said Maggie. "I think he must have meant that when he wrote about our getting ready for him."

" That's a good idea," replied Hugh ; " yes, that would do, but the question is, what *are* we to set about ? How do we know what he'd like ?" And Hugh put a fresh log on the fire.

" O Hugh, there are his letters. He's said so much in them that would tell us. I've got one in my pocket that I was reading before school, and I hadn't time to put it back then, and forgot afterwards. Hugh, I've got a plan. We all have some letters of our own that father's written to ourselves on our birth-days, and at odd times. There'd be enough to last us till he comes home if we were to read one together every week, on Saturdays after school ; and they'd help to tell us about get-ting ready for his coming back."

" I've got eight," replied Hugh ; " I've lost two or three."

" And I've got five," continued Jamie.

" And mother's keeping four of mine for me," answered little Nannie ; " but they're very short. I know them almost by heart."

" Never mind that," said Maggie ; " they'll help us all the same. I have ten quite safe. Let me see—ten, and eight, and five, and

four—twenty-seven altogether. They'll last
us for all the weeks, even if we begin to-day.
When it's fine on Saturdays, we could come
here or into the wood, or even in the garden
and read the letter, one belonging to each of
us, turn about; and if it's wet, we'll sit over
the fire and Hugh shall read it, because he
reads best."

Maggie was very fond of making little
plans for the future, and of painting them in
pleasant colours, and this was one after her
own heart. Sometimes the rest differed from
her, but in this instance all agreed, and settled
how nice it would be to feel that one letter
less would show that the longed for day was
one week nearer.

"Now for the first letter!" exclaimed Hugh.
"Maggie, read it yourself, you'll know better
how, as it's your own."

"It was written nearly two years ago,"
answered his sister, drawing it from her
pocket—"for our eleventh birth-day, Hugh."

They all settled themselves to listen, and a
bright little party they were, and picturesquely
grouped, too, round the fire which burnt
bravely and well. Hugh with his dark eyes

so like his father's, Mary Christie said, and
with his open face, and brave, honest expression of countenance.   Maggie, with her fair
hair, and shy, timid glance, and with a bright
colour which came and went, telling quite
plainly what passed in her mind, and making
it quite unnecessary to look for the further
testimony with which her large deep blue eyes
corroborated everything it told, sat next to
him, with the cherished letter in her hand.
Nannie looked up inquiringly to catch the
words as they fell, her round, baby face con-
trasting curiously with Jamie's delicately cut,
pale features which told far more than his
little sister's of his Indian birth and delicate
babyhood.

"It's plain to read," said Maggie, "father
writes so clear."

"MY VERY DEAR LITTLE MAGGIE,—

"This ought to reach you near about your birth-day,
and I shall write to Hugh besides.   Whenever your birth-day
comes, it makes me sad to think that so many have passed without my seeing you, and I wonder how many more will pass before I *do* see you again.   I can remember you so well the day I
wished you good-bye.   You were such a dear wee thing, and
you had your arms round my neck, and cried just as if you knew
I was going from you, and I often wonder now what you are
like, and wish I had your arms round my neck again.   We sol-

diers have such hard lives, that it makes us think more of home and all the kith and kin over the sea. I have been thinking what I *want* you to be, my dear Maggie, and on your birth-day you must find out whether you are like this, and if not, ask God to make you so.

" I want you to be *truthful* in word and deed. A person who is deceiving is a coward before God and man, and there is nothing so disgraceful to a soldier as to be called a coward. I want you to be *gentle*, for I should be very sorry that my dear little girl were to be like the poor children who stray about here in the barracks, and are so rough and rude; and besides, Jesus was gentle like a lamb.

" I want you to be *obedient*—first of all to God, then to your mother and your teachers. The Bible is God's word of command, and remember, my dear Maggie, we have promised for you to fight manfully under the banner of Jesus Christ, and to follow his will to your life's end.

" I want you to be *diligent*, because idle people are always unhappy ones, and because God tells us to be diligent. There is nothing that we soldiers dread out here so much as having nothing to do, and I am sure you will be always happy if you have something useful in work, or lessons, or play in hand.

" Lastly, my dear Maggie, I want you to be *humble*. First to be humble before God, to feel how sinful you are, and how you can do nothing to save yourself, but must come as a guilty sinner to wash in the blood of Jesus. And then the thought of how sinful you are before God must make you humble to every one. If you are praised, you must remember that he knows your sinfulness within; if you are reproved, do not be proud or angry, because you must feel how much he sees that deserves reproof far more than you receive. My dear Maggie, often think that a proud look is an abomination to the Lord, and that he that humbleth himself shall be exalted. If we think of how humble Jesus was, it will help to make us humble.

" And now, my dear Maggie, I must write no more, as I have told all news to mother in my letter to her. I want you to read

on your birth-day in the sixth chapter of Ephesians, beginning
at the eleventh verse, and to ask God to give you all his armour
for the new year. You are a soldier's daughter before the world,
but I want you to be a real soldier before Jesus Christ, and he
will help you to fight manfully if you ask him.

"With my best prayers and love I must conclude, so no more
this time from your affectionate father,

"H. M. CHRISTIE."

All the little party were quite silent for a
few minutes when Maggie had ended. Hugh
was the first to speak. "I'm afraid what you
said was true, Maggie ; he'll expect us to be
better than we are."

"But we've got six months to try in," replied his sister, hopefully. "I think it's
hardest to me to be diligent. I'm often lazy ;
but now I shall remember better, I hope."

"I'm diligent every now and then for a
flare up," said Hugh, "but not steady at it.
But it's all easier than being humble and gentle,
as father says ; that sounds more for girls.
Maggie, what do you mean by looking so ?"

"There's a little bit in the letter that you
had the same day as this that I remember,
Hugh, because father said we were to read
each other's ; it was that the truly brave are
always truly gentle."

"Yes, I remember; and then he says, too, that he should like to think we were living for others, and showing love to Christ so. Dear me, Maggie, we're a long way off from all this."

Jamie began to count on his fingers: "Humble, obedient, gentle, diligent, truthful, living for others—and six months for it all."

"It would take six years," sighed Nannie; "we couldn't ask father to wait a little, could we?"

Nannie was well laughed at, especially as she had thought that the six months would never come to an end; and then they were all silent again, and busied themselves with the fire.

"I've thought of a plan," said Maggie, looking up quickly; "listen, Hugh, and don't throw stones for a minute. Let us each set to work about something that father would like us to do, and try and get it done in time to show him—something that'll please him very much indeed, and that'll help to make us what he wants."

"I don't see what there is to be done," replied her brother; "we must be good to mother, I suppose."

"Yes," replied Maggie, "but something particular, I mean. Hugh, I know what would please father more than anything! What day comes in the end of June?"

"Midsummer day," suggested Hugh.

"No, a greater day than that for us; prize day, Hugh."

"Well, I expect to get a prize," replied Hugh. "I got the writing prize this year, and geography last year in my class."

"No, not those prizes—I don't mean *those*; but, Hugh, what's the prize father would like you best to have?"

Her brother did not reply at first; then he said half sheepishly, "You mean the conduct prize for the school; but, Maggie, there's no use trying."

"Why not? You're so clever, Hugh—far cleverer than most of the boys, and you'd have had it last year if it hadn't been for—"

Here Maggie paused, lest she should call up unpleasant thoughts; but her brother took her up. "If it hadn't been for thrashing Will

Carson, and for helping in the row when that old miser's windows were broke."

"If we were to set to work together to try," continued Maggie, "it would help to make us care for just the things father wants us to be—humble, and gentle, and diligent, and all the rest."

Hugh did not answer, but began whistling "Annie Laurie," accompanying himself by a repeated series of performances of the dick, duck, and drake description, which, though they might not have appeared encouraging to any one else, made Maggie quite sure that he was thinking of what she said. Suddenly he stopped, and sat down again by her side.

"Maggie," he exclaimed, "you're right. I'll get the conduct prize; I'll determine. There's nothing would please father half so well, or Mr. Malcolm either; and I mind him. I'll get it among the boys, and you among the girls."

"You forget; I can't get it among the girls," she replied; "it's partly for regular attendance, and mother wants me at home washing and baking days, so I've no chance. It'll be harder for me to be contented not to try, and to stay at home and help mother; but then father'd be better pleased I did so, than if I went to school and got the prize."

"Then mother'll tell him, Maggie, about you, and think how glad he'll be if I show him I've followed his advice, and have a prize," and Hugh looked as triumphant as if his success were complete. It was just like him to take up an idea suddenly, and to be quite elated as he carried it out in prospect; but then he was not persevering, and often became as suddenly depressed. Maggie knew this, and was almost sorry he should adopt her plan so warmly in a moment.

"Even suppose you shouldn't win it," she began.

"But I'm determined, Maggie; it's not suppose—"

"Yes, dear Hugh, only—"

"Only what?"

"Why, after all, Hugh, father would care more for seeing gentleness, and love, and diligence in our hearts, than even our getting the prize, and I think we must try not so much for the prize—"

"There, Maggie, that's just like you; first

proposing a plan, and then when I take it up, throwing cold water on it."

"No, Hugh; you won't listen to me; I'd give anything for you to have the prize, and father'd be delighted ; but I mean to say he'd care more for your having *deserved* it, than for the honour, and then that he'd wish us to try and deserve it, not so much for the prize, as for the sake of pleasing God."

Hugh was silent, and seemed half put out, but he recovered himself after a minute. "I believe you're right, Maggie," he said; "you girls always twist things so queerly. But I see what you mean. We oughtn't to try more to please father than to please Jesus Christ, who died for us. It would be best, if one could, to put away the thinking about the prize, and to try to be good because it's right. And after all," he added, "there's no reason why the prize shouldn't come of itself."

Maggie crept up close to her brother, glad at what he had said about doing right for right's sake, and yet with a wee bit of a smile on her lips at the finishing up of his sentence. Then she began again,—

"I've thought some time, ever since the

letter came, of what I ought to do. When we
were going out of school that morning, and
Mr. Malcolm had been speaking so to the
children, I spied poor little Alice Donald
sitting by herself in the play-ground, and crying so that the tears were all over her black
frock.   And then when I put my arms round
her neck, and asked her what ailed her, all she
could say was, "*My* father never came home,
Maggie."   And then after a minute she said
that she was very unhappy now, and that
Mrs. Carson, who had charge of her, says she
can't keep her at school any longer (though
Mr. Malcolm will give her schooling free), because she hasn't any clothes fit.   The parish
gives her something for keeping little Alice,
because, after all, she's a sort of an aunt, or
second cousin, and there's no one else to look
after her.   But it's not enough to clothe her
fit to be seen; and Mrs. Carson says she's
too poor to dress her respectable, and she
won't let her come ragged.   And, Hugh, I
thought then, when I was so happy, of the
day when the fishing-boat was wrecked, and
of how little Ailie never saw her father again
as we shall see ours; and I thought that I

could work if mother'd cut out, and so I
could tell God how I thanked him by trying
to make Ailie's clothes for her. I didn't like
to say anything till I'd asked mother; but
she said I might try, so that I didn't give up
my own work, and that she'd let me have
some of Nannie's things when she grew too
big for them, and that she'd cut them for me
to fit Ailie, who's so wee for her age. And I
thought I could save some of my money and
help them out, and that perhaps Mrs. Malcolm
would now and then give me a cast-off frock
of Miss Bessie's, and that others would help,
if God would help me to try." And Maggie
looked wistfully at Hugh.

"It's very good, Maggie, but it won't be
exactly for father."

"Oh, but, Hugh, father writes about living
for others, and he'd rather I worked for a poor
little orphan than any one else. Don't say
that, please."

"And you hate needlework?" said Jamie.

"God is giving our father back to us,
Jamie," she answered, "and even if I hated
it worse, there oughtn't to be anything
we wouldn't do for Him; and then when

I think of what he says about the least of
his brethren, I'm sure it's the thing for me
to do."

"Now it's my turn," said Jamie; "what
will there be for me?"

Hugh whistled, as his wont was when his
wits were set to work, and Jamie looked
inquiringly at Maggie, who was supplying the
fire.

"There s my hen," he said; "it lays beauti-
fully; I'll save up my egg money, and buy a
present for father,—a large pocket-handker-
chief like our master's, with the flags of all
nations upon it;" and Jamie looked triumphant.

"It seems to me that the hen would have
all the work, and not you," said Hugh.

"Well, it's my money," answered Jamie;
"I should think—"

"We all have something for making
money," interrupted his sister, who saw that
Jamie did not like Hugh to laugh at his
plan; "you have a hen, and Hugh has
his pigeons, and I have the bees, and Nannie—"

"Has flowers and a rabbit," suggested

Nannie, who saw that Maggie did not know exactly how to bring her in.

"Yes, has flowers that she can make something by; and we might all put our money together next June, and buy something for father that he'd like. We might save all our money, and get a great deal—perhaps a pound, and buy something great."

"Capital," said Hugh, "let's agree to it!"

"But for me alone," persisted Jamie, "what am *I* to do against he comes?"

"Make a cherry-net," said Hugh; "you know how."

"I don't like that; besides, it's not the sort of thing."

"You might fill a book with sums," suggested Maggie; "but I'm afraid that won't be what you'd like either."

"Mind the garden, Jamie," whispered Nannie.

"Well, I declare that wouldn't be a bad plan," exclaimed her sister. "Jamie, if you were to work hard, and get Mr. Scott to advise you, and the neighbours to give you some plants, and every one to give a help, you might get the front garden by the door

4

beautiful by June.   Of course you couldn't do
the hard work ; but you could weed, and
plant, and water, and keep the beds clear, and
we'd all help, only it should be your charge."

Jamie brightened up.   " Would mother let
me ? " he asked.

" Oh, mother'd be sure to," replied his
sister ; " and when people know it's to be got
right for father to come back to, they'll all
give a hand."

" It's too much for Jamie," said Hugh ;
" he'd better not take it ; I'd be the best."

" Only you work for Mr. Malcolm sometimes, and you'll have to work hard for the
prize, and we must all help in the back garden," answered Maggie, with a private pressure
upon her brother's hand, to which he rather
doubtfully yielded; and the matter remained
to be referred to their mother.   " Now,
Nannie, for you."

Jamie had at once begun to take counsel
with his little sister as to the floral decorations which he was to supply for his father's
return; but she would only settle the W of
the " welcome," as she listened to Hugh's proposition for herself.

"Father'll expect you to read, Nannie," he said.

"But I can't much," she replied soberly. "I know how to read 'Tom was a good lad,' and 'The cat ate a rat,' in the spelling-book, and things of that sort."

"I wonder what sort of rat was eaten and dished up in a spelling-book," said Hugh; "but listen to my plan. We'll help you, Nannie, every day after play-time, or at home, and if you try very much, you'll be able to read a chapter in the Bible for father the night he comes home."

Nannie looked delighted. "Do you think I shall be able, Maggie?" she said.

"I'm sure you will," replied her sister, "and that'll please him better than all, when he knows what pains you've taken to get on for his sake. What a good thought of Hugh's!"

"Yes," said Nannie, "before we go to bed, father'll ask for a chapter, and mother's not to know anything about my having learnt so quick; and she'll say, 'My dear' (she'll call him My dear, won't she?) 'Hugh shall read it.' And then Hugh will say, 'Nannie'll read

it;' and then mother will say 'She can't;' and
then you mustn't laugh, Jamie, and I'll say,
' Let me try ;' and father'll take me on his lap,
and I'll begin ; what chapter shall it be,
Maggie ? "

" Something about somebody coming home
like him," said Hugh.

" The prodigal son ?" suggested Jamie inquiringly.

" Oh no, Jamie," interposed Maggie; " not
that."

" About Jacob coming to Joseph's the only
thing I remember about a father coming to
his children," said Hugh musingly; " and
father won't be like him, and we shan't be
like his sons."

" I've thought," said Maggie brightening;
" father told me his favourite chapter in one
of his letters—it's the tenth of John, about
the Good Shepherd, and that's easy reading."

" Yes, that'll do," said Nannie, " and you
and Hugh will have heard me all the long
words before, only you mustn't tell me when
the time comes.   And then when I've read it
through—all that part about the Shepherd—
he and mother'll be so pleased, and he'll know

that I've tried to please him, though I couldn't do such grand things as the rest."

"Well, we've had a long talk," said Hugh; "but it's nice to have settled everything, and we can all set to work at once, which is a good thing for making the time short. Perhaps this day six months father'll be with us here on the beach, and we'll show him where everything was settled for us to do."

"Yes," rejoined Maggie; "and we must try and go steadily to work,—not giving up when we get tired, and helping each other to be gentle, and diligent, and patient, and we know God will help us if we ask him."

"I think that when we're going to be cross, or tired, or giving up," said Hugh, "one of us must just say quietly, '*Father's coming home,*' and that'll make us remember."

"Yes," said Maggie, "let us agree to it. Hugh, what a good planner you are!"

It never crossed Maggie's mind that she had planned more than any one else, and had helped her brothers by her gentle words and thoughts to resolutions which would not have occurred to them but for her; but it was very much her way to keep self in the background, for far more than the rest she had been led by the heavenly Teacher into the knowledge of the truth into which he guides all who seek his guidance, and she was daily learning at the foot of the cross the lessons of deep humility which are never to be fully learnt until we make that our abiding-place.

The sun dipped gloriously into the sea as the four children turned homewards, with their baskets full of shells, and their minds full of the projected plans which were in part confided to and approved by their mother.

And when Maggie awoke the next morning with the thought that she was to begin working that day, and when with it came the re membrance of the letter and the fear confided to Hugh lest her father should after all be disappointed in her, Hugh's own words sounded back most pleasantly on her ears: "But he *must* love us, Maggie, even though we're not quite good; we're his children, and he can't help it."

III.

Maggie's Plan.

" Inasmuch as ye did it unto the least of these, my brethren, ye did it unto me."

Maggie's Plan.

THE winter holidays passed swiftly by, and the Christmas and New Year's seasons gained brightness in the eyes of the Christie children, as they said to each other, that ere the next New Year's morning their father would be with them in the Airie home.

They were all pursuing the plans which had been laid down by common consent in the council held on the beach, and to all of which, as far as they had been confided to her, their mother had given her willing concurrence, being well satisfied that the brothers and sisters should have been stirred up to find, in the prospect of their father's return, such an inspiring motive for active employment. Maggie's prophecy that the time would pass very quickly was coming quite true; and the

Saturday readings of the precious letters, which wonderfully kept alive the zeal and energy of the four, seemed to follow each other so closely that Jamie and Nannie could hardly believe that these weeks contained the same number of days as those which had preceded the arrival of the good news.

Maggie's self-appointed task required the most perseverance, as she undertook it with the firm determination that it was not to interfere with her usual school and household duties, which latter included assistance to her mother in washing, and baking, and in keeping all the linen of the family in repair. Mary Christie would sometimes offer to have some of these duties done by other hands; but Maggie always persisted that she could make time for her mother and for Alice too. And, indeed, what with getting up earlier in the morning, and with giving spare minutes and most of her play-time to the work, she contrived by the end of the holidays to produce a neat black frock and cloak, partly made out of an old dress of her mother's, and kindly cut out for her by Mrs. Mackay, the school-mistress, who gave her some very useful teaching in this department, and told her that she might always seek her assistance in her plans for the little orphan.

That was a glad day for Alice when Maggie called at Mrs. Carson's house with the bundle, which Hugh helped her to carry. It was the last afternoon of the holidays, and poor little Ailie, whose school friends were the only ones she really loved, was sitting wearily by the side of the cradle rocking a fretful baby which would not go to sleep. The house was a dismal one, a long way from the Christie's; and Mrs. Carson had a temper which made it more dismal still. When Maggie appeared at the door, Alice sprang from her seat, and hiding her face in the clothes of her gentle visitor, burst into a fit of crying.

"Hush, Ailie; what's the matter?" said Maggie gently, and asking leave to sit down. "Don't cry so, darling. I've come to brighten you, and to bring you a New Year's box."

But Alice cried still. "There's no making nothing of her, Maggie Christie," said Mrs. Carson in a loud voice, and ceasing for a moment to rinse the clothes which lay in con-

fusion around her. "It'd be as much good
talking to that table. Look when I will,
there she is cry, cry, cry, day and night.
Why, as I says, stirring about's the thing for
her, and there's enough to do here, I know, to
keep every one stirring. But I put her to
scour, and clean, and nurse the baby, and
mind the fire, from morning till night, and it's
all the same. She'd like to go to school the
morrow, I know, and I never doubt that's
what she's crying for; but as I says, where's
the clothes to come from? Will and the baby's
enough to keep in clothes besides her; and
I'm not going to have the minister's wife calling upon me, as she did before about Sally
that's dead, to ask why she can't come tidy.
It'd be a good riddance of a crying child if she
went, I'll warrant, though."

"O Maggie, it's for father I'm crying,"
whispered Ailie tremulously. "I mind his
face when they took him out of the water; it
comes back to me nights when they think I'm
asleep, and then the crying comes again, and
she scolds me. He said he'd come home to
me after three months, and I counted the days
—they made ninety two altogether; and then

he never came;" and little Alice cried faster
than ever.

Maggie's tears fell fast too. *Her* father
was coming to her; suppose that she had
a sorrow like Ailie's—oh, it was too dreadful
a thought to keep in her mind! And then
this little one had no friends to love her, no
kind mother's voice to soothe her, nothing but
the hard sound of reproach from morning till
night; and Maggie clasped Ailie tightly in her
arms, as if she would have shielded her from
it all.

"I had hoped," sobbed Ailie, as she saw
that Mrs. Carson had left the room, "that
aunt wouldn't have stood out about not let-
ting me go to school; but my clothes wear
out so with house work, and Mrs. Malcolm's
speaking years ago offended her so. O
Maggie, I'm miserable here. Couldn't I get
away? No one comes out so far, and I'm kept
minding the baby, and it's so heavy to lift."

"Look, Ailie," said Maggie, taking the
bundle which Hugh had delivered over to her
before they reached the house, as he did not
personally care to go near the Carsons' cottage; "will these clothes do?"

Ailie silently clasped her hands in amazement. "O Maggie, they can't be for me!" she said. "How *did* you get them? Are they really to be mine?"

"Yes, Ailie, if your aunt will let you come to school."

Alice seemed too bewildered to speak.

"Ailie, darling, I'll tell you about them," said Maggie gently, laying the parcel on the table, and taking the little orphan on her lap. "They're from me, in a way—that is, they're my work, and with my love. You know, Ailie, *my* father's coming home. I thought one day he was dead, and then I had that dreadful feeling in my heart which you've had too. And then the letter came, and I felt as if I must do something to tell our Father in heaven how thankful I was. And then I saw you, and God seemed to tell me that was my work. So you see it's more from Him than from me; it's sent to you by the Father of the fatherless, Ailie. And now you'll be able to come to school again, and learn about him."

Little Alice did not speak, but she *looked* quite enough to please Maggie, who began to explain matters further.

"You must put this frock and cloak on before you come to school, and keep them very neat, and take them off directly you come home. This is a hood made out of a larger one of mine. You see it just fits you, Ailie; and you must tie it close down these cold days. And then the white pinafore's to be brought to school on Monday, and left with your work, and you're to put it on every day before prayers; and then mother says you may bring it to us on Saturdays to wash, and you can call for it the next Monday morning."

Maggie had barely finished when Mrs. Carson came in.

"Look, aunt, what she's brought," said Alice timidly.

"These for you, Alice!" she exclaimed. "Well, some folks must have more time on their hands than I have, I reckon. Ah! the stuff's coarse enough, I see. How much a yard was it, Maggie?"

"It's not new stuff," replied Maggie gently; "I couldn't have afforded that. It's made out of a dress of mother's."

"Oh! old things made new again; I understand. I thought it wasn't all new. But

I'm not to be after washing pinafores for you, Alice, I promise you."

"Maggie says that she'll wash it after school, aunt," said little Ailie nervously.

"I thought as much," replied her aunt sharply. "You'll be crying again to go to school. I doubt whether you can be let to go, though. Who's to mind the baby?"

"You said I'd be a good riddance, aunt," faltered little Alice, whose hope lay in those hardly-sounding words.

"It's only for school I've made these clothes for Alice," rejoined Maggie, more firmly than usual, for she saw that Mrs. Carson had been making lack of clothes an excuse for retaining Alice as a little maid-of-all-work; and her gentle spirit was roused for the moment. "If you can't let her come, I must take them back to mother."

Poor little Alice! her lips quivered with anxiety. Maggie had come in like a messenger of hope. Would she give up so soon, and leave her again?

"It's very hard," resumed her aunt coldly, " to have a child left on one's hands like this. She eats more than I get for her, and there's no thanks for anything one does. If her father'd have minded what I said, he'd have looked to himself, and gone in a Letter boat, and then he'd have been back to mind his own."

Oh, how Maggie's heart warmed towards the little pale-faced orphan by her side, whose sensitive feelings were so continually chilled by speeches like these!

"I must not stay," she said quietly; "but if you please, Mrs. Carson, to decide; because I'll tell Mrs. Mackay on Monday if Alice is not to come. It was she who helped me to cut out the clothes."

Mrs. Carson hesitated for a minute. Then she said in a careless tone, "She may go on Monday if she likes; but if she goes tearing her things, why, I'm not going to have new ones to make for her."

If Maggie had worked for thanks or gratitude on the part of Ailie's aunt, she would have turned away with damped ardour, and with determinations to do no more. But hers were higher motives. The earthly father and the heavenly Father were in her thoughts; and though she felt a little disappointed that

5

Alice should return no answer when she bent down to whisper that, when the frock was worn out, there would be another made, and that there was a warm petticoat nearly finished for her, she left the cottage door to join Hugh for a walk home through thick, drizzling rain, with a happy feeling in her heart, as if she had heard Jesus whispering, "Inasmuch as ye have done it unto the least of these my brethren, ye have done it unto me."

She had hardly joined her brother when she heard the sound of little feet pattering after her through the gathering darkness, and Alice sprang to her with her face uplifted for a good-bye kiss.

"O Maggie," she said, "I was afraid to say anything before aunt, for fear I'd seem too glad, and she wouldn't let me go. But thank you very much, Maggie; you've made me so much happier, and you never answered all she said; and I'll try and be good like you. And, O Maggie! I'll pray every day that *your* father may come safe home to you (I can't do anything else but love you), and then he'll know how good you've been to me."

And fearful of being scolded for her absence, Alice ran back again, only with something very like a sob at the end of the thanks.

"You've made the best beginning of us all, Maggie," said Hugh; "you've worked all the holidays so hard. And I'm quite sure now that you've thought of the thing father'd like most after all."

Maggie did not answer for a minute. Then she replied, "O Hugh, Hugh! it's the *keeping on* that we must try for. We'll help each other not to weary in well-doing."

IV.

Difficulties.

"Oh, to be in England,
  Now that April's there;
  And whoever wakes in England,
  Sees some morning, unaware,
  That the lowest boughs and the brushwood sheaf
  Round the elm-tree bole are in tiny leaf;
  While the chaffinch sings on the orchard bough
  In England—now!"

BROWNING.

Difficulties.

FRESH news arrived from the anxiously
looked for father, and each letter was
brighter than the last, as each marked
the nearer advance of the day which
was to unite him to his family.

It was on a fine, warm morning in
the beginning of April that Maggie, work in
hand, sat by the window of her home, while
her thoughts busily occupied themselves with
the despatch that morning received and which
had been penned by her father on the day of
his embarkation for his native land. It was
to be his last, he said; for they would not
again hear from him until he should appear in
person to receive the welcome awaiting him.
The letter, which had travelled by the short
route from India, was seven weeks old, and
Maggie calculated that in ten more he might

be expected to follow it to Airie. And as she
sat diligently at work, making rapid progress
in a dark grey frock for little Alice, which
had, after much contrivance, been fitted for
her out of an old one which Nannie had out-
grown, she very willingly received the congratulations of the merry birds without, who
came under the window to sing out to the
kindly lassie who fed them so constantly, and
sang so cheerily in chorus with them that they
were glad, very glad indeed. And then the
sunbeams came dancing in too, to tell her the
same thing; and one or two ambassador-bees
came on a message from the whole hive—
Maggie knew they did—to hum out a pleasant sort of a song, which was intended to
express to her that they would be willing to
furnish the best honey in their power when
the looked-for day should appear, and that
they took a particular interest in everything
that gave satisfaction to a young maiden
whose diligent habits they had much pleasure
in observing.

So Maggie received all these congratulations with due appreciation and regard, and
then found herself repeating over and over in

her mind the last words of her father's letter,
" And now I am almost beginning to believe
that I am coming home." And then came
some pleasant thoughts of prospering plans.
Ailie's grey habiliment might have appeared
nothing more than a coarse grey frock to the
unconcerned spectator, but in Maggie's eyes it
was a very marvel of execution. No stitch
had been taken in it unaccompanied by the
bright thought of the day that was coming,
and she could have shown you the exact place
at which she had been working when Mr.
Malcolm had called in to say that he had
had heard of Maggie's undertaking in behalf
of little Alice Donald, and that if she remained
at school to the end of the half-year, he would
recommend her for admission into the small
orphanage established long ago in Airie by a
benevolent individual, and to which female or-
phans were admitted on condition of their having belonged for two years to the parish school.
And then Mr. Malcolm went on to say that
if it had not been for Maggie, Alice would
have had no chance of such good fortune,
especially as the vacancy had been quite sudden and unforeseen; and he told her that God

often prospers the humble, persevering efforts
of his children, made for his sake, by carrying
them on unexpectedly in a way little dreamt
of at first; and that when Maggie would see
the little one for whom she had worked so
perseveringly, fed, and clothed, and provided
for until she should be placed in service,
according to the rules of the orphanage, she
would have a testimony, besides that of His
word, to assure her that her heavenly Father
had not disdained to accept the endeavours
which she had made for him, and had granted
them success.

And Maggie, with all her delight and con-
fusion which she could only testify in courtesies
and " Oh, thank you, sirs," for very bewilder-
ment, felt as if she must not let Mr. Malcolm
go without speaking out quite, quite honestly.
So at the seventh courtesy she took courage to
falter out,—

" But indeed, sir, I've not done much—
that's to say, mother and Mrs. Mackay helped
me for the stuff, and the pinafores are very
coarse if you look close at them, sir; the last
one was made out of the best part of a sheet
which was mostly worn-out; there's a darn in

one corner of it—the left-hand side, close to the hem. And then, sir, Mr. Malcolm, I *did* want partly to please Jesus, and to work for his sake; but besides, I felt very sorry for Ailie, and *my* father was coming home, sir— that was a great deal the reason for my beginning." And the colour came and went upon Maggie's cheeks as she spoke out so shyly and hesitatingly.

Mr. Malcolm smiled quite encouragingly when she had done, and said he liked her being honest; and he wrote a few words on a little slip of paper, which he told her she was to open the first time that she felt rather inclined to tire of her work; and that happened when the gathering-thread broke, just as she began to sew on the skirt of the grey frock, and all the gathers had to be done over again. Then Maggie peeped at the little folded paper which she had been forbidden to open before, and there were the very words she wanted,— "*Be not weary in well-doing;*" and underneath the golden promise, "*My grace is sufficient for thee.*" And these words speeded her on, and so did the loving gratitude of little Alice herself, who so cried for joy at the pro-

spect of being removed from Mrs. Carson, and
for gratitude to Maggie, who had given so
much time and trouble for her, that her friend
felt quite overwhelmed.

So these were pleasant thoughts to the little
workwoman as she began to finish off the task
in hand, on the bright April morning of which
we have spoken. How delighted her father
would be to know that his Maggie had been
trying to follow his counsel to her, to live
for others! And then Hugh was getting on
bravely at school. His whole heart was set
upon winning the prize for good conduct,
which was to tell Hugh the elder that his boy
had been working to please him. He had as
yet had neither late mark nor bad-conduct
mark, and Mr. Malcolm had told his mother
that he was giving more satisfaction than in
any previous year. So this was all good news.

Nannie's chapter was progressing, too.
She had learnt out of school-hours almost all
the hard words. She could read " *Shepherd* "
without stopping to spell it, and was gradually
mastering the long sentences, which became
easier every day, for the good reason that unconsciously she was learning the oft-repeated

chapter by heart,—a way of conquering diffi-
culties upon which her brother and sister had
hardly calculated, but in which her quick
ear and quick memory served her in good stead.
Nannie was quite triumphant, and could
hardly be persuaded to keep her secret
from her mother, who was not admitted to it
as it was to be a complete surprise. Sometimes, indeed, the little one's energies flagged,
and she was inclined to be cross and pettish ;
but the magic words, "*Father's coming home !*"
softly whispered by Maggie, had wonderful
effect, and that not only as concerned the
chapter. Fretful ways and cross tempers were
regarded as more serious enemies than they had
ever appeared before, and the prospect of
his return and approval was observed by the
children's mother to correct, outwardly at
least, many a wayward inclination, and many
a careless habit which might have refused to
disappear before repeated admonitions.

But underneath most joy, anticipated and
even real, there is a drawback,—greater or
less, as the case may be, but a drawback still.
And so it was with Maggie's pleasant thoughts
this morning. For it must be remembered that

in her small person were combined many important offices. She was not only Maggie, chief-helper at home, under baker and laundry-maid to the family, and needle-woman to little Ailie Donald, but she was further prime counsellor, conjointly with Hugh, concerning the preparations for her father's return—lady-superintendent, in fact, of all the plans in course of operation, and the diligent promoter of the same. And the little queen-bee was uneasy respecting one of the working-bees who had promised much, but who had become strangely careless and fitful in his conduct, and whose sympathy in the prospects and interests of the rest had of late unaccountably flagged. And over and over again the question repeated itself to her mind, "What can have come over Jamie?"

And the question was one not easily to be dismissed. With it Maggie threaded her needle, and with it worked on silently. What had come over Jamie? During the winter he had talked so much of his garden undertakings, had studied all that he could understand of sundry books with many coloured plates, which Mr. Scott, Mr. Malcolm's

gardener, had lent him, and had made arrangements with Maggie for a series of floral adorn-
ments, which, though planned on too large a
scale for execution, told well for his zeal in the
common interest. And until within the last
few weeks, he had gone on very steadily, not
shrinking from the troublesome work of clearing the ground, and digging the beds, in which
more than one of his elder school-fellows
helped the brothers and sisters. But Maggie
knew that the promising appearance which
the garden now presented, was but very little
due to Jamie. Some new and wrong influence was over him which was clearer to her
eyes and to Hugh's, than to their mother's,
who was so much within doors, and who, besides, was sometimes too busy to notice many
things which were obvious to the elder children. She had, indeed, been surprised when
Mr. Evans had called to inquire how it was
that Jamie's lessons were now so imperfectly
learnt, in consequence of which she had given
the boy plenty of good advice, which he
did not apparently care much to receive,
and had desired that he should bring his
books in doors, and learn his lessons under

her eye, which proceeding he much resented.
But Hugh and Maggie felt that he cared less
and less to belong to them. Nannie, who
had always looked up to him as her hero
and adviser, found herself so coldly and
harshly received that she shrank timidly from
his company. He spent his play-hours with
a set of elder boys, who, Maggie fancied, tried
to win him away from Hugh, by making him
think himself too old and manly to be led by
his brother, and of which set Will Carson
was the leader. Jamie no longer looked
bright and happy. The whisper of the three
magic words which acted as such a stimulus
upon the others had no effect upon him; and,
in school at the bottom of his class, at home,
the source of vexation to his mother, sisters,
and brother, he was a complete puzzle to them
all.

Maggie was deep in her thoughts upon this
subject, and had just repeated to herself
Hugh's words, spoken only the evening before,
"You may depend on it that Carson and
his set have got hold of Jamie, and are leading him wrong," when the door opened, and
Hugh himself walked in.

The countenance with which Hugh entered
caused his sister to cease her employment
and inquire, "What *can* be the matter?"
Her brother did not answer. His lips were
firmly compressed with a half-proud, half-
indignant expression, and his face wore the
look which a boy's face usually wears when
he is sorely inclined to cry, and, at the same
time, desires to convey the impression that if
you think he has any disposition to turn soft,
you are very much mistaken indeed. "Hugh!"
exclaimed Maggie again, "something has
happened wrong; *do* tell me what it is."

He darted from her as she came up to him,
and, running hastily up the stairs to the little
bedroom occupied by himself and Jamie,
slammed the door in a manner which told
Maggie that she had better not follow. Sadly
and wonderingly she folded up the frock,
completed now, with the exception of the neat
little mourning tucker with which she always
thought it desirable to finish off the dress of
the orphan child, and then, looking at the
clock, she saw that it was time to lay the
cloth for dinner, and to expect Jamie and
Nannie home from school and her mother

from the market. The children came first—
Nannie before her brother.

"What can be the matter?" she exclaimed,
running up the steps from the garden gate;
"they say something's been wrong in the
boys' school, and I can't get Jamie to tell me
anything, except that Hugh's got into a scrape.
Isn't he home yet?"

"Yes, he's home," replied her sister, "but
don't be going to him. Nannie, there *is*
something wrong, I'm afraid."

Jamie, meantime, had appeared in the distance, coming slowly up the road. He did
not hurry on seeing his sisters; rather the
reverse; for, when arrived at the top of the
steps, he began to practise jumping the entire
flight, although it had been satisfactorily
proved in the full family committee that he
had attained to the dignity of being able by
general consent to accomplish that feat, and
the question of his proficiency had been completely set at rest.

Maggie went down to him. "What's
wrong with Hugh?" she inquired, as they
walked up the path together.

"Some row about the marks," was the reply ; "they say it'll take the shine out of his chance of a prize."

"It can't be !" answered Maggie, almost indignantly ; "I'm sure it's not Hugh—there's some mistake——"

"Mr. Evans is in the mistake, and Mr. Malcolm, too, if it *is* a mistake," rejoined her brother.

"*If*," exclaimed Maggie, "it's no *if*; I'd take Hugh's word in a minute against every-thing, however bad it might appear." And, with these words, she left the children, and ran to the door of Hugh's little bed-chamber.

She opened it very gently, and, looking exactly in a contrary direction from where her brother stood as she knew that he did not like her to know when he had been crying, walked to the window and remained there for some minutes without speaking, while Hugh, with his back to her, plaited a piece of whip-cord and unplaited it again as methodically and diligently as if he had come up stairs and shut himself up for no other purpose.

"How was it, Hugh ?" asked Maggie after a minute's silence.

"How was what ?" was the gruff reply.

"You know, Hughie; do tell *me*—what has been making you—"

"Cry," was on the tip of her tongue, but like a wise little lassie she substituted "vexed."

"Who said I was vexed?"

Maggie knew that Hugh, like most other boys, was always slightly ferocious when in fear of breaking down, so she did not answer, feeling perfectly sure that he would speak again in a minute if left alone.

"Who said I was vexed?" he repeated, as she had expected, after a pause.

"I knew it when I saw you," answered Maggie; "and the children said there had been something wrong at school."

Hugh did not answer, but having again unplaited the whip-cord, began to pull it to pieces in a most deliberate and pains-taking manner.

"It makes me miserable to see you vexed," said Maggie, coming up to him and putting her arm round his neck; "Hugh, *do* tell me everything."

"Don't bother," was the reply, as he removed himself further from her; "you girls are always like that."

Maggie did not answer for a minute; then, after vainly waiting, she called up her final resource. "You won't let me help you," she said sorrowfully, "though I would if I could; but remember, Hughie, father's——"

"I wish he wasn't——at least not now;" and Maggie heard that his voice was thick and tremulous.

"O Hugh! to think of *your* saying that!" she replied hurriedly, "you who've been trying so hard to please him!"

"Yes, and all to have him told when he comes home that I'm a cheat, and a sneak, and a liar, and a——"

"Hugh! who could? nobody could——"

"It seems that somebody could," he interrupted angrily, and then suddenly flinging away the whip-cord, and with it the fortifications of pride and indignant reserve which he all at once found himself obliged to abandon, the boy threw himself on his bed, sobbing out with difficulty, "And I had been trying so hard to please him!"

Maggie knew she need not go then, so she knelt down by the bed-side close to him, and said softly every now and then, "Don't cry, Hughie; don't cry so."

As might have been expected, these words did not immediately stay the torrent, but after a few minutes, the sobs became less frequent, and he was willing—anxious, indeed—to let out his sorrow to the faithful little sister by his side. Of course, he began at the wrong end. "It's Will Carson," he exclaimed angrily, "it's all his doing ; I knew he'd try and prevent my getting the prize. He's got Jamie away into his set ; he's boasted that he'd keep above me in the school ; he worries Alice Donald because he thinks we care for her. I'm sure that he could clear it up !"

"Clear what up?" inquired Maggie gently.

"Why, they say that I've been at the mark-book," was the burning reply ; "they say it, all of them—master, and the rest ; and even Mr. Malcolm's been got on their side."

"You !" exclaimed Maggie in amazement ; "they can't."

"They do, though. It was yesterday after school. I had got down in geography two or three times this week—down below Will Carson who's taken to it lately for a flare-up, and because he's trying against me for the geography prize. I was vexed enough at losing the

marks for I knew they'd make quite a differ-
ence in the summing up for the examination,
and besides, I don't know how, but I've got
a notion that he hadn't got up fairly—"

"O Hugh! we mustn't suspect—it's not
like you."

"I don't care—I *do* suspect, only I've not
said it to any one; I don't think he has
any real work in him. Mr. Evans was surprised, I know he was. He said he was glad
to see Carson getting on so quickly, far
better than he had expected. And then he
said he must have guessed at the questions by
magic to have prepared so well."

"And how did Will look?"

"Just like a great, staring—" Hugh could
not think of any word that expressed his
meaning and so left the rest to be understood.

He stopped for a moment and then continued:—"Well, after school, I asked Mr.
Evans to let me stay in and finish colouring
a map that was to be shown up at the end of
the month to Mr. Malcolm and the visitors.
He had promised to lend me his colours when
I had to finish it; and he said I might, and

that when I was ready, I was to come across
to his house for the colour-box. I was for
more than half an hour doing the pen-and-ink
work, and then I left it on the desk and went
over to the master's house. I had to wait a
few minutes before he could find a key to
open the box. He said he'd lost the bunch
which had the right key on it, besides the
key of his school-desk. Then I went back
and finished the map, and ran home quick to
dinner, and Reynolds who had been to his
home, spoke to me in the play-ground as I
went by."

"Yes, but what has that to do with
the—with what's wrong?" asked his sister
anxiously.

"Why, this morning, Mr. Malcolm came
into school, and looked on, and said just by
accident to Mr. Evans that he was glad Carson had got on in geography so well, and that
from the monthly marks that had been sent
in yesterday to him, he saw he was nearly up
to Hugh Christie. So then Mr. Evans said
he was beyond me, and that Mr. Malcolm
must have made some mistake. And then
Mr. Malcolm felt for ever so long in his pocket,

and at last found the paper, and showed Mr.
Evans that my marks were set down higher
than Will's. Master said it was a mistake,
and called Reynolds the teacher, who copies
out the monthly marks, and asked him when
he had copied them. He said yesterday just
before afternoon school, and that he had copied
them from the monthly paper, which brought
the marks down to the day before yesterday,
and which lay in the master's desk as usual;
and that after he had copied them, he had
compared the two papers, and torn up the old
one. Mr. Evans asked him if he was sure
that he had copied them exactly, and he said
he was quite sure. Then Mr. Evans said he
had a copy in his own house of all the marks,
that he kept every day, and had kept up to
yesterday morning, a paper which we boys did
not know of, at least I didn't. And so he
went and brought it in, and Reynolds fished
out the torn bits of the last monthly paper
from some dust-hole, and stuck them together,
and showed that it was the same as Mr. Malcolm's, and that it brought me out first, while
Mr. Evans put Carson first in geography.
Then there was a long fuss over it, and it was

plain that the figures had been very neatly altered, just as if it was done by some one who wanted to take in Reynolds who always copies the paper for Mr. Malcolm, and by some one, too, who knew that the old paper was not kept after the copy was made. And then some blue colour was found on the back of the paper, just the same shade as my map, and as if it had been smudged by some one in a hurry who had paint on their fingers, and the figures were like mine—just exactly—and—and—" Hugh's indignation and sorrow were getting the better of him again, and Maggie was nearly as bad; but after a minute, he went on :—" It was clear that it had been done between morning and afternoon schools, and nobody seemed to have been in the room but me, and it was so unlucky my having asked to stay in that one morning, when generally I'm in such a hurry to get off to play. Everything seemed to say it was me."

" But couldn't some one have come in when you went to Mr. Evans for the colours, and then have gone to the desk and altered the marks ?"

" That's what must have been," replied her

brother; "but then why should he? for I'm sure it's Carson, or some one he's sent. It would seem to be against himself. I don't suppose he knows—I'm sure I didn't—that it's from Mr. Evans' register, copied from the monthly paper, that the prize marks are added up. I thought it was always from Mr. Malcolm's, and that Mr. Evans only kept the conduct marks. Besides, no one knew that the keys were lost but me; and the master's desk is almost always kept locked. It's so hard to make out. If it hadn't been that Mr. Malcolm's so particular, and sometimes comes at the end of the month to speak about the marks it wouldn't have come out so soon."

"But how strange it was that Reynolds should find the paper that had been torn up?"

"Yes; two or three of the boys went to look for it with him—Carson too. He seemed quite anxious it should be found. I never expected to get the geography prize against him. He's so clever—clever and deep, and he always seems so good before every one that has anything to do with the school."

"Hugh, don't speak so. I know it's very hard for you to feel right when such things have happened, but, you know, it may be some one else."

The boy did not answer for a minute, then he burst out again, "And father coming home, too! They'll make him believe it; there's no proving I didn't do it. But I didn't—I don't care what they say—I didn't do it! They all looked solemn, and Mr. Malcolm said he couldn't believe it even then, if the proof hadn't been so very strong; but that he would call and speak to mother. He said he knew I had been trying for prizes to please my father, and that a sudden temptation must have overcome me; and then he preached a sermon to the rest, and I was the text, and Carson had a meek look like what he puts on for Sundays when he thinks the clergyman's eye is on him, and I knew he was as glad as possible. And so when Mr. Malcolm had done, and they took ever so long examining the rest, and trying to find out whether any one knew that Mr. Evans kept a fair copy of the marks; when he had done, I felt I must speak, and so I said out, 'I'm sorry, sir, you can't trust me—I thought you

would have known me better; but my father
will believe me, sir, when he comes home; at
least, I hope he will.' And then, Maggie, I
walked out, with my head up; I felt proud.
I know I did, but I couldn't help it."

"O Hugh! I wonder you weren't afraid—
and to Mr. Malcolm too!"

"I'm not like a girl to be afraid when I've
done no harm," was the reply; "1 daresay they've
told him what I said outside—that I'd never
go inside the school again until I was made
clear, and I won't."

"But won't mother make you? I'm afraid,
Hugh, it isn't right to say that."

"There's no use preaching, Maggie; if you
were made out to be what they've made me
out to be, you'd feel the same. Mother will
never make me go back before father comes
home."

"And all our plans," sighed his sister—"all
our plans that were to have made his coming
so glad,—O Hugh!"

Hugh did not reply. Poor fellow! he could
not. Manly as he was, this sudden trouble
seemed more than he could bear. Almost
unconsciously, the idea of gratifying his re-

turning father's affection and pride by his successful exertions had been the sometimes acknowledged, but still more frequently the unacknowledged stimulus to his now for the first time really persevering endeavours ; and the thought that he was unable to clear himself from the imputation of a fault which in a soldier's sight would be absolutely without excuse, filled him with disappointment and indignation. He had not his sister's even temper and disposition. When elated, his spirits were unquenchable, and, on the other hand, when suddenly cast down, he could not rise or see any hope through the gloom of depression.

It was a dismal dinner-table. The bright sunbeams which had said so many pleasant things to Maggie in the morning seemed to be intruders now ; and little Nannie's remarks about some merry-making which was to take place when her father should return were brought to an untimely end by a touch from her sister, who succeeded in checking the little chatterer as completely as a parrot is extinguished when a dark covering is thrown over its cage.

Mary Christie was, as might have been expected, deeply hurt and distressed. She placed implicit trust in her boy's word, and could hardly be expected to realize the extreme difficulty of clearing him from the charge. The fault had plainly been committed. It was one which could not be too strongly condemned, and which, occurring publicly in a school, demanded the most public and determined exposure and reprobation, and—here came the difficulty—it seemed nobody's interest, except Hugh's, to have committed it. It was well known how anxious he was for the prize, and how hard he was working for it. He himself had been obliged to allow that he thought that the marks which decided the assignation of the prize were added up from the monthly papers in Mr. Malcom's keeping, and all the boys knew that it was Reynolds' business to copy them, who having nothing to do with the elder classes, and being entirely occupied with the youngest children in the adjacent class-room, acted merely mechanically, and of course could not know that the marks were false. It seemed evident that the boy who had tampered with the figures, trusted to the well-known

custom of the destruction, or at least abandon-
ment, of the old monthly papers when the fair
copy was taken, and Hugh was the only boy
in the school-room who had been observed to
be present when, after the dismissal, Mr. Evans
had desired Reynolds to remember to copy out
the marks of the month which had ended the
day before, and had told him that he would
find the desk unlocked, as he had mislaid his
keys.   Hugh declared that he had heard some
one else in the class-room at the time, who
must have been a listener to the order so given;
but then there was the grave fact to prove
against him that after hearing this, he had
asked leave to stay in, and this was far from
being his usual habit.   Reynolds must have
visited the desk very soon after Hugh had left
the school-room ; and then there was another
stronger proof against the boy—a proof which
he himself could not but see, that even sup-
posing a rival—Carson it might be—capable
of altering the marks, this of all other months
would have been the least likely to have been
selected by him for such a purpose as clearly
the alteration would tell *for* Hugh and against
himself.

It was a most perplexing affair. Sensible woman though she was, his mother could not but be so far influenced by her feelings, as to repeat that Hugh's simple denial should be considered as sufficient by the authorities. Her pride—and her motherly pride in her children was not small—was deeply touched; and when Hugh—wilfully, rather, but very earnestly— pleaded that he should not return to school, but should study on by himself till his father returned, or till his character should be cleared, she did not deny his request.

For the first time in his life Mr. Malcolm, on calling at the cottage that afternoon, experienced a reception more distantly respectful than cordial. He was not surprised, but sat for some time alone with Mrs. Christie laying all the circumstances before her. Even now, he said, he could hardly bring himself to believe her boy capable of the fault, so highly had he esteemed his honest and upright character. But then—and the *but* would return—how strong was the proof against him. "Yes, it was strong," Mary owned, but then *she* was sure it was not her Hugh who had done this —*she* knew him far too well to believe it, and

7

she had thought Mr. Malcolm knew him too. He had been anxious for the prize, she allowed; it was to please his father; and she knew that he had been vexed at losing his place in geography; but for her husband's son to have acted as Hugh was suspected to have acted was manifestly impossible. Mr. Malcolm was very kind and considerate, but he appeared to Mary Christie's eyes to be inclined to sympathize, and sympathy was what she did not wish for just then from him. He told her that it had been repeated to him that Hugh did not wish to return to the school until he should have been cleared—that of course, as this had not been said in school, he could take no further notice of it than to say that he hoped she would use her influence to prevent his carrying out his desire, as he felt it might be most injurious to the boy himself, as well as, by example, to others.

Mary Christie answered respectfully but sorrowfully that she did not know what to say—that she felt most gratefully all the kindness her children had received and the exceeding value of the instruction given at the schools, but that it would be very hard for her boy who had never had a reproach on his name to go back with the credit of such conduct as that of which he was accused, and with the consciousness that he was looked down upon by every child in the parish. If he did not like to go, she thought she must leave it for his father to determine, and that, until his return, Hugh must judge and decide for himself. She told Mr. Malcolm how hard he had been working with the hope of offering a joyful greeting to his father, and although promising that her influence should be on the side of his return to school, still refused to exercise any authority in the matter.

It was not to be wondered at that the good mother should indulge in a shower of tears after her visitor's departure, and Mr. Malcolm himself was sorely perplexed and troubled in spirit. Hugh was in the garden, and took off his hat respectfully as he passed, but with a very different expression of countenance from that with which he usually greeted the minister, who, however, called him to his side, and kept him for a few minutes in conversation.

At its conclusion poor Hugh was more

grieved than ever. Mr. Malcolm had shown him seriously but affectionately how those who think themselves the strongest may be carried away by sudden temptation, and how lying, stealing, or taking from another his due, and dishonour both to his earthly and his heavenly Father had been exercised in this matter—in fact, the boy felt that if there had been time, all the ten commandments would have appeared to be involved. And when he spoke so kindly, Hugh's heart—a warm and impulsive heart it was—felt again the strong glow of affection for one who had always been his kind friend, even though now he was suspected by him. But when Mr. Malcolm parted, with the hope that he would some day work up again to the position he had held in the school and regain the confidence of masters and boys, the proud spirit of the soldier's son flashed into his face, and the "Thank you, sir," which followed, had more than a tinge of bitterness.

Hugh lay down that night indignantly resolved not to re-enter the school until he should have been proved innocent.

And Mr. Malcolm, who, with his strong

respect for the value of circumstantial evidence, had most unwillingly taken the part which he had been constrained to take, exclaimed to himself while he thought the matter over, "Everything goes to prove the boy guilty, and yet I believe him to be as innocent in the matter as myself. At all events, I'll leave no effort untried to clear him."

If, indeed, William Carson had been the means of bringing this trouble among the Christies, he had, for a time at all events, well succeeded in his object. His dislike to Hugh had begun from the time at which it had appeared evident that his younger school-fellow would render his position as head of the class and of the sports a doubtful one. This feeling had increased month by month, and reached a climax when, some months before the opening of our story, Hugh, having detected his rival attempting to bully his little sister, rushed to the rescue, and closing upon him suddenly, used his advantage to such purpose that Carson then and there received marks of corporeal punishment which branded his dislike to Christie deeper than ever into his soul. Hugh got into disgrace for taking the law so immediately into his own hands, and offered to make up with Carson. But the latter was heard to remark in a low voice that he would be revenged; and, incomprehensible as seemed the form of revenge, Hugh felt sure that it was now that he was keeping his word.

V.

Hugh and Maggie in Council.

"Content to trust Him day by day,
With every anxious care ; —
Content to fill the lowest place,
And think of Jesus there."

Hugh and Maggie in Council.

THE morning which succeeded the events of our last chapter was calm and bright—so bright that it might have been laid claim to by the summer as its own property, which, for some unknown cause, had been produced by its predecessor, spring. Fair, however, as was all without, the members of the Christie family rose gloomily to their daily avocations. Mary Christie, worthy woman though she was, was inclined a be a little peevish and vexed, and told Hugh that if he had been more careful not to make enemies, he wouldn't have had to suspect any one of bringing him into trouble; which remark, as it happened to contain much wholesome truth, Hugh did not relish. He, poor boy, did not know what to make of his time. This was

the quarterly holiday for the school; and had
not this trouble come upon him, he would
not have known how to make enough of it.
He would have been busy in the garden and
with his bees during the morning, to say
nothing of working up his lessons with a view
to maintaining his position in his class; and
then, in the afternoon, there would have been
an expedition to the sea-shore, or some game
of hare and hounds or paper-chase, in which
he would have been the prime chief and ring-
leader to all the boys in the village.   Now
he walked listlessly about, moodily and half-
mechanically arranging matters in the flower-
beds for a few minutes, then relinquishing
this occupation, and taking up another with
equal want of interest.   Maggie knew that
any attempt at sympathy would be resented in
Hugh's present frame of mind, and so went
about her usual morning's work.   But the
birds heard no echo to their chorus from her
lips, and Nannie, who, after working at a
coarse duster which her mother gave her to
hem, in the most exemplary manner, came
voluntarily to propose a reading lesson with a
view to the great undertaking in hand, was

surprised at receiving a refusal for the first time from her elder sister, who told her to take her book up stairs and get on by herself, and above all, not to let Hugh hear her talking about it.

Jamie looked white and ill. He had gone out after complaining of a head-ache and of inability to eat his breakfast; but when his mother inquired where he was going, his only reply was, "out towards the copse."

"He's going to the Carsons," was Maggie's remark as he disappeared; "mother, I wish you wouldn't let him keep company so with them. I'm sure Will's leading him wrong."

"Leave him alone," was Mary Christie's reply; "he want's a walk, and the fresh air'll do him good. I'm not afraid of their leading him wrong, poor lad, and there's no use worretting for no good."

His sister did not answer, but privately determined to make another great effort to wean the boy from the influence which was leading him from them all, and which offered as its only compensation for loss of regard and standing both at home and at school, the society and fitful friendship of a few boys older and bigger than himself. The time, however, was not then. Jamie came back to dinner; but the meal was a hurried one, as Mrs. Christie wanted Hugh to take a message for her to a house about two miles off—a commission which he was glad to execute, as it would take him for some time away from everybody and everything at home,—and only Maggie noticed the traces of tears on the little boy's cheeks, and the timid shrinking manner in which he spoke and acted. Hugh was delayed after all in his expedition, as some neighbours came in for a chat with his mother; and then, having begun to mend Nannie's rabbit-hutch, respecting which the little maiden was most anxious, he was unable to leave it before it was completed, and the afternoon was already tolerably advanced when he started for the little hamlet to which Mary Christie's parcel was to be conveyed.

"Mother," said Maggie, as Hugh silently walked down the garden walk, without, as usual, bounding to the bottom of the steps with a flying leap, and whistling cheerily on his way, "mother, mightn't I go too?"

"There's no reason why you shouldn't,"

was the reply; " unless it's too far for you.
It'll be company for Hugh, poor fellow, and
your work's done for to-day.   Don't hurry
home," she added, when, after a minute's
interval, Maggie appeared in her straw bonnet
and gray cloak; " I'll keep your tea for you
both, and maybe you'll come home something
brighter."

Hugh was walking soberly along by the
side of the brook when he felt a hand on his
shoulder and saw Maggie by his side.   It
was a lovely afternoon.   The vegetation was
unusually advanced for the season of the year,
and the birds had been recently getting up a
chorus entitled " Hail, smiling Spring," of
which they had a rehearsal just as the brother
and sister were passing under the trees; so
that even Hugh, who was in no mood for
music at that time, could not help stopping to
listen to the sweet notes which chimed in so
melodiously with the murmur of the brook,
which in every sense performed a flowing
accompaniment.   And although neither he nor
Maggie imagined it for a moment, they, themselves, looked very spring-like, with their young
twin faces—alike, and yet so different; and

with earnestness and hope already partially
developed in their clear brows, to be still more
fully read and traced there when they should
have touched their summer-time, and when the
fruit should have followed the blossoms. Yes,
they were spring-like, although to them the day
was a cloudy one, so cloudy that for some
minutes they walked on silently as if neither
liked to interrupt the thoughts of the other,
although both knew what those thoughts were.

At last Maggie began, "Hugh, I've come
to walk with you—you don't mind?"

"No, you can if you like," was the moody
reply, gruff-sounding, but as good as Maggie
expected.

Their way lay past the door of Mrs. Carson's house, which looked so dismal and untidy that the passer-by wondered how any
one should be utterly careless respecting his
habitation when Nature was busied in making hers so green and fair. Nobody was at
the door, nor could Maggie's eye discover any
sign of Ailie's presence on the premises,
though a greeting from her would have been
very cheery just then. But as they turned
down a lane which led them by the shortest

way to their destination, they saw Will Carson himself, lounging on a gate as if he did
not know what to make of his holiday. He
turned his back upon them as they came up,
and walked away. Maggie hoped that he
did not see Hugh's averted countenance.

"I'd go out of the way to avoid him," was
the remark that met her ear.

"It's partly about him I wanted to speak
to you, Hughie," she rejoined rather timidly;
"couldn't you get to feel right to him?"

"Yes; when he's spoilt all I was trying
for, and made everything miserable."

"But you're not sure it was he who did it,
Hugh; you can't be sure till it's proved."

"I *am* sure," was the rejoinder, and for a
few minutes she did not know what to say.
Then, like a brave little sister, she returned
to the charge.

"Hugh, I've come out to get a quiet talk
with you. I know it must be very hard for
you to feel kind to any one, even me, just
now when everything's gone wrong; but
don't be angry with me about what I'm going
to say."

"Well, go on."

"It's about—I wanted to ask you—don't you think you ought to go back to school?" And Maggie took breath as if she had accomplished these words with great effort.

"I *am* going," was the cool reply.

"Dear Hugh," was the quick rejoinder. "I'm so glad. I was afraid you'd stand out about it, and it would grieve Mr. Malcolm, and —."

"I'm going back, but not now. When Mr. Malcolm has cleared me, Maggie, I'll go back, and to my own place."

"That's just what I was afraid of—your waiting away. I know it would be very, very hard for you to go now, and to be thought less of than you have been; but, Hugh, I've been thinking —"

"That you'd like me to be a mean-spirited, sneaking fellow, whom any one might put upon without having a word in return."

"Hugh, you know how I care about your being looked up to and thought of; but I've been going it over and over in my mind, and I can't help thinking you'll prove your being clear more by going back now, and besides —"

"And I can't help thinking that I'll prove

it best by showing that my character isn't being taken for nothing. Wouldn't it be nice for me to go back and see the conduct-prize that was to have been mine given to Carson, and the geography prize too, most likely; and for me to hear Mr. Malcolm say to father, 'I hope your boy'll gain it some day yet.' And then wouldn't it be nice to see Carson's face? He's never had a conduct-prize in his life, and he's been keeping wonderfully good in the sight of pastors and masters since he knew I was bent on the prize for father. No truant-playing now; no riding Mr. Malcolm's horse round the fields when he's been the other way. Oh no! he's quite a pattern, and every one will be 'delighted at the change.' "

"Hugh, dear Hugh, I wish you wouldn't speak so. It's not like you. You're cross sometimes, but not like this; couldn't you try to feel different, although it's so hard?"

"Then don't expect me to give in, Maggie. You're a girl, and girls are different. One thought of Will's face next Monday, when he'd see me at the bottom of the class, would prevent me from ever going back till I'm righted."

His sister did not reply for a few moments. Then she said, softly, "And one thought of Jesus Christ's face when he humbled himself to the death of the cross and said, 'Father, forgive them,' would make you feel right, Hughie."

A few steps more brought the pair to their destination, and leaving his sister at the gate of the small farm-yard at which they had arrived, Hugh carried his mother's parcel to the house, and rejoined Maggie after a short interval.

"Which way shall we go home?" he inquired soberly.

"Let us go by the cliffs, Hugh; it's longer, but mother said we needn't hurry, and then we shall see the sunset." So they started for their homeward walk.

Now it must be known that Maggie, with all her gentleness, was as determined a little lassie as ever was seen, once, as in this instance, she had made up her mind that her object was a right one. And it must also be known that, almost unconsciously to herself, she had more influence with Hugh than any other person on earth. Her twin brother, from whom she had never been separated, and with whom alone of all her family her earliest years of childhood had been spent, she clung to him with that true, fond affection, which being for the most part purely unselfish in its nature, is more often found to proceed from sisters to brothers than from brothers to sisters. Maggie, too, was older in character than her brother. Scholars in the school of Jesus Christ gain much maturity even in the early days of their teaching, and with the wisdom from on high comes oftentimes a calm, quiet discernment and discretion which, from its being the result of a constant endeavour to live singly to God's glory, puzzles those who know not the secret spring of this outward working in no small degree.

Like a careful pilot who well knows the waters through which he is steering, Maggie had made her way amongst various outlying rocks and breakers of Hugh's present wayward mood into the deeper and stiller current which she knew to be beyond them. And now she left her words to find their own soundings, whilst, from her forbearing to continue the discussion, and from her diligence in

finding violets in the hedgerows on either side
of the lane, it might have been supposed that
she had abandoned the subject altogether.

Hugh did not stop to look for flowers, but
walked slowly on.   After an interval of some
minutes, he broke the silence,—

"What makes you wish for me to go back
to school now?"

"Because I think that going back and
bearing up against all that'll worry will prove
your being innocent more than anything else,"
was the reply; "at least that's part of the
reason."

"And what's the rest?"

Maggie seemed doubtful whether she should
proceed any further; but there was nothing
to discourage her in her brother's face—she
had taken the soundings carefully.   "Besides,
Hugh, it seems to me that God has let this
trial come, because—because, perhaps, we all
made too sure of ourselves (she need not have
included herself) about pleasing father; perhaps we thought more of the outward prize
and of appearing to be good than we did
about pleasing God.   Don't you think, Hughie,
that if God has let this come to make you

think of working more for him and to please
him, it seems wrong to say you won't bear
it. He can clear you when he chooses."
And she looked wistfully into his face.

"It all sounds very good, Maggie," replied
Hugh, sadly, but without any harsh tone in
his voice. "It all sounds very true; but you
don't know—you can't know what it feels
like to be called a coward, or mean-spirited, or
sneaking; and that's what they will call me
if I go back tamely, and put up with a charge
that hasn't a word of truth in it."

"Perhaps I don't," replied his sister; "and
yet I think I should feel it more for you than
you would for yourself; but then, who is it
you're afraid of? Not Mr. Malcolm. I believe he thinks you clear now, though he
can't prove it; but he'll respect you all the
more if he sees you're like what father said in
his last letter to you—great enough to be
humble; so will Mr. Evans; so will Reynolds,
and all the best boys who told you they felt
sure you'd come out clear; so would —

"Carson!" interposed her brother, bitterly.

"Yes, Hugh! so would Carson in the end
—not at first. I believe Carson has had

something to do with it, and I can't help fancying that poor little Jamie guesses at it too. But, Hugh, it would be a better victory than winning the prize if you could win over the boy you can't bear now."

"Win *him!* He's not worth trying for. What good should I do by winning him?"

"You would overcome evil with good, and you'd have a feeling in your heart that you wouldn't exchange for any prize."

"I'm not at all so sure of that. I don't think anything could ever make me feel love, or care for that—I don't know what to call him."

"One thing would, Hughie."

"What?"

"Thinking of Jesus would. 'Consider Him who endured such contradiction of sinners against himself, lest ye be weary and faint in your minds.' I've sometimes thought that nothing will help us so to get over disliking people as thinking of the part we had in the sins which He bore instead of us."

"You're better than I am, Maggie; I don" have these thoughts." Rocks, reefs, and breakers had all been cleared now, and cleared successfully.

" I usen't to, Hugh; but now they come much oftener. They make dull days even so pleasant, because one has Jesus always to please."

" If I thought like you do, Maggie, I think I'd go back to school even now," said Hugh, meditatively, and leaning over a stile that separated the termination of the lane from the open space of smooth, short turf which stretched along the coast at the summit of the cliffs overhanging the sea-beach.

" Don't you remember that same letter of father's," she continued, pursuing her advantage, " the one we read together in the apple-tree last week, and how much he wrote in it of the brave soldier in his regiment who was willing to be sneered and laughed at for reading his Bible, and for refusing to drink and to break the Sabbath, and how, when some one asked him what kept him so easy about it all, he showed him that verse, 'If any man *suffer as a Christian* let him not be ashamed, but let him glorify God.' "

" I'm not a soldier."

" Yes, you are, Hughie, a soldier of Jesus, and this is the battle-time—the real, hard battle-time—and He's looking on and longing for you to win."

Hugh did not answer, but sprang over the stile and walked to the edge of the cliff, calling to his sister to follow. It was a glorious sunset scene. The throne-room of the declining monarch was hung with all glorious draperies of purple and gold, while sky and ocean had combined to reflect the splendours of the slowly-descending orb which sank to rest

> "Like a martial chief when the battle is won
> Most triumphing where he dies."

Untutored and simple as they were, the brother and sister had a genuine and true sense of the glories of creation, and in that presence they stood almost spell-bound until slowly, slowly the glory faded away, and the silvery moon, which, pale and unacknowledged, had waited the departure of her royal predecessor in the empire of the heavens to assert her gentler sway, began to make her soft presence visible.

"It's time we were going," said Hugh at last.

"Yes," replied his sister, drawing her cloak round her, "but first let us look down the cliffs. There's just the place where we came the day the good news arrived from father, and where we lit the fire, and made the plans."

"Yes," replied poor Hugh; "and the plans have all melted away, except yours and Nannie's."

"No, Hugh; yours hasn't a bit. Don't you remember saying that it wasn't for the prize you intended to try, but to *deserve* the prize, and that was what father would like. And don't you remember how we settled that we wern't to think so much of doing things as of being what he wished us to be—like Jesus. And you're trying to be that, Hugh, and though you mayn't have the praise of men just now, yet you have the opportunity sent you of becoming greater in God's sight, because 'he that humbleth himself shall be exalted;' and though we care so much for pleasing our dear father on his return, O Hughie, it's worth more to take the trial which our heavenly Father sends—He who gave his Son for us."

"I don't know what to think," half soliloquized Hugh, as they walked together along the cliffs; "if I begin, I'm not likely to keep

on humble and good.   Directly they say anything I know I shall flare up."

"You wouldn't, if you could hear Jesus say
you were to bear it for him ; or, if he were to
stand before you and point to his hands and
feet and remind you of the scorn he bore for
us."

"But then, Maggie, those thoughts don't
come at the right time.   They come in church,
or when one's looking at the sunset, or at
night, or with father's letters ; but not between the time when a fellow gets up a laugh
at you and you give it him back."

"Once you begin, Hughie, you go upon
God's strength ; and he's true to his promise
of sending it.   I thought nearly all last night
about this, and it made me very unhappy.
And then it seemed to me that it must have
been sent to try whether you would be willing to take Christ's yoke and learn of him who
was meek and lowly in heart.   And then I
got out of bed by Nannie's side, and I asked
him to make you willing, and to show you
that the lowest place is a happy one if Jesus
is in it with you ; and I thought of that hymn
which mother sometimes says,—

'Content to fill the lowest place,
And think of Jesus there;'

and I prayed that I might say some words, Hughie, out of the Bible, and that you might begin to try for something better than the prize,—that you might try to find Jesus in the low place, and perhaps to win Carson by love."

"Maggie, you're as good as a clergyman," was her brother's rather surprised remark; "you'd make a good one."

"Don't say that, Hugh. I can't talk to any one, not even mother, as I do to you. But I love you so much, and you know we two have always belonged most to each other."

"Maggie," he replied, as their path began slightly to descend, "I think I'll go to school on Monday, but," as he noticed the sweet smile which stole to her face, "but I can't be gracious to Carson. I won't thrash him, though I could, and I won't even look angry at him; but I can't try to care for him. It's too much to expect."

"Look, they've left the gate open; come this way," she replied quietly, as, turning into a little descending path to the left, and going down a few irregular and moss-grown steps, she entered, through a half-open gate, a small enclosure projecting beyond the cliff, although a good deal below its level, and commanding a full view of the bay, now lit up by the clear, reflected moonlight. Hugh followed, wondering why she went.

It was a little piece of consecrated ground, —consecrated long years before as a burial place for shipwrecked mariners drowned on that dangerous coast. The time of its having been set aside for that purpose was beyond the memory of the oldest inhabitant of the neighbourhood, but the story ran that the family of some rich lord in years gone by had found him thrown lifeless on the beach below, at the close of a day whose morning had seen him start forth in his gay vessel in full strength and vigour ; and that they had caused this little corner of his domain to be consecrated as a place for his burial, and for that of the poor, strange seamen who in after years should share his fate. So the tale was told; and, whether true or not in its origin, it had become customary to make use of this as the place of interment for drowned mariners, the number of

THE SEA-SIDE GRAVE-YARD.

"The moonlight made them easily discernible, and the brother and sister
read them, as they stood there hand in hand."—Page 125.

whom, however, had become fewer every year, so that, until just lately, the little sea-side grave-yard had not been opened for years. It was very very still. The grass was long, and the graves, five or six only in number, were for the most part overgrown, and the evening lights made it look yet sadder and stiller than usual.

"Maggie, why are you going there?" asked Hugh; "we ought to be getting home."

She did not reply, but led him almost to the edge of the little promontory, to a newly made grave, apart from the rest, and showing some evidences of care in its less neglected appearance. There was a rough head-stone, and on it a few words, chiselled by an evidently unskilful hand. The moonlight made them easily discernible, and the brother and sister read them, as they stood there hand in hand :—

MICHAEL DONALD,
AGED 48.

JAMES ARNE,
AGED 37.

Drowned, Nov. 2, 18—, near the shore below.

"*Be ye also ready; for in such an hour as ye think not the Son of Man cometh.*"
"*To him that overcometh will I give a crown of life.*"

Underneath was a rudely sculptured image of a ship, tossing on the waves, and the two children looked silently upon it, and then far beyond over the bay. The west was glowing yet, even as though orders had been left by the departed monarch of day that the tapestries of purple and gold which adorned his antechambers should remain until overhung with the dark draperies of night. In and out, where the moonbeams timidly fell as if searching for waters that should reflect their light, a little white skiff wound along, like the ship upon the grave-stone, the image of the short, fleeting life of tossings and turmoils which must be ours before we can reach the haven of rest. And any one who had thoughtfully beheld the scene, and marked the young, earnest faces of the twin brother and sister as they stood, would have likened them, too, to fair, newly-launched barks, and would have prayed that they might follow no uncertain course through the waves of "this troublesome world,"—that heaven-bound gales might bear them towards the homeward destination, and that the heavings and tossings of this changeful life might only further their progress towards the desired haven and harbour.

"Why have you come here, Maggie?" repeated Hugh in a voice unconsciously lowered in its tone.

"I can't tell quite, Hugh; I wanted you to come. I think that being brought near to look at death makes one feel everything else so small, and—and, Hughie, it says, '*To him that overcometh will I give a crown of life;*' and if death were to come suddenly to you as it did to Alice Donald's father, you would be glad to have overcome and to have forgiven."

Hugh did not reply. Maggie's words were very simple, and perhaps would have made little impression upon him at another time; but here—here by the new-made grave of the lonely seamen—in the quiet, still evening hour, and with the rudely cut but solemn words, "*Be ye also ready,*" before his eyes; here—away from all the world beside and close to death, a still-sounding voice found its way to the boy's heart.

"*Be ye also ready!*" Yes; he had thought much of being ready to greet his father,—the father now homeward-bound to join them all;

but was he getting ready for Jesus Christ?
"I *will* humble myself," replied a voice from
within. "I will humble myself, and bear up,
and go back—but I *can't* forgive!" And
then again the voice, "*Be ye also ready,*" spoke
from the tomb-stone, and with it another
which said, "*If ye forgive not men their trespasses, how shall your heavenly Father forgive
you your trespasses?*" And Hugh Christie
felt that he was not "ready" then; that he
needed forgiveness of sins before he could meet
death—forgiveness for the sake of One whose
righteousness was more worthy than his own;
and there came over him a rush of remembrance of the story of Calvary, and of a head
crowned with thorns, and of a cry, "Father,
forgive them!" and there sounded, like a clear
bugle-call in his ear, the word of Him who
had prayed that prayer for *him*, saying, "To
him that overcometh will *I* give a crown of
life;" and his eyes seemed suddenly to discover, by a new light, the glories of a path
which had opened before him of forgiveness
and lowliness, the end of which was lost in a
flood of light; and he turned to his sister with
the words for which she had prayed, "Mag-

gie, if Jesus will help me, I think I can forgive."

The walk home was a silent one ; both were content that it should be so. Hugh, once determined to follow the footsteps of Him whose voice had called him aside from the fair and easy path of outward prosperity and esteem, into a narrower track of lowliness and meekness, seriously sought counsel within to guide his steps and steady his progress. Negative forgiveness—a mere abstaining from injury to the boy who was his enemy, was, he felt, not alone what was required of him ; it was not that which had been shown to men, and which, "*while we were yet sinners*," caused Christ to die for us. No ; he felt that more was needed, and that *more* he desired to obtain where alone it could be obtained.

And Maggie, with the sweet, quiet smile upon her lips, was full of hope—a trembling hope—for the dear, dear brother by her side. She only trusted that he might not become wearied at the outset by the trials of the new path he had chosen,—that he might find sweet flowers in the Valley of Humiliation, that the

9

bright hope of pleasing a dearer than an earthly father might be in his heart through every difficulty.

So they came home with these thoughts in their minds, and found their mother looking out for them at the gate.

"A runaway pair you are!" she said cheerily, as they returned; "why, I expected you home an hour ago."

"You told us not to hurry, mother."

"No, I'm glad you've had the walk. There's what's good for you in the oven; if you're not hungry you ought to be after your walk."

There was something very bright and cheery in the motherly home-greeting. Hugh and Maggie felt it so.

"Mother," said Hugh, as they rose from family prayer before separating for the night, "I'll go to school on Monday morning as usual."

"God bless you there, my boy," she said affectionately; "I remember what your father said once when he heard of one of our great generals who had fought his way into the enemy's garrison and gained the day; he said,

'That's a brave man, and there'll be many a high-sounding name given him ; and yet how strange it seems that in God's sight, *he that ruleth his spirit is better than he that taketh a city.*'"

And these words sounded pleasantly in Hugh's ears that night.

VI.

Getting Ready in Earnest.

" He that is down need fear no fall,
He that is low no pride,
He that is humble ever shall
Have God to be his guide."

PILGRIM'S PROGRESS.

Getting Ready in Earnest.

HE kept his promise, though when on the Monday morning he stood for a moment outside the school door, half undecided whether he should enter, pride made one more hard fight within, and he felt almost inclined to retreat. But "*to him that overcometh*" sounded in Hugh's ears, and his face was calm and undisturbed as he quietly took his place at the bottom of the class, of which for many months he had been the head, whilst Carson, in a whisper quite audible to his quick ears, said something about upstarts going down in the world. But there is a verse in the Bible in which it is said that God will keep his people in the pavilion of his presence from the strife of tongues, and Hugh was just beginning to understand its meaning. Maggie's

words had sunk into his mind, " One thought
of Jesus Christ's face when he humbled himself to the death of the cross will make you
feel right ; " and that thought which on the
Sabbath-day he had been praying to be en-
abled to remember, kept him peaceful under
circumstances to which a week before his
proud spirit would have refused to yield.
Hugh was for the first time trying a great ex-
periment,—whether really and truly heavenly
strength and peace are given in answer to
prayer, to those who are in earnest in seeking
to do God's will, or not ; and he found it true.
He had never before felt how the common
duties of daily life may become elevated and
ennobled when performed " as unto the Lord;"
and though the master, he thought, looked
coldly on him, and many of the boys con-
temptuously, Hugh, at the bottom of his class,
gained an insight into true peace and happiness such as he had never known before when
its acknowledged head.   At the conclusion of
lessons, Carson, now placed first, collected the
books as usual, and gave them to Hugh to
put away in the shelves,—the office always
performed by the lowest boy in the class.

"Make haste," he added, in a tone which tempted the other to let the books fall to the ground, "I can't have the class kept waiting by you." Hugh took them silently and put them away in the next room. There was an indignant look in his eye which told that the quiet contempt had not passed unheeded, but when he returned it had disappeared.

As might be expected, his demeanour caused some surprise amongst his school-fellows, who watched with curiosity the boy who had so long been their leader, and who now appeared degraded from his position. It was so entirely unexpected that it caused some suspicion; in fact, several lingered after school-time with the expectation of witnessing "a blow up" between Christie and Carson. The latter confided to several of his followers that Hugh was "coming it meek and humble" before the master, that he might get a favourite, and perhaps have another chance for the prize; but that he knew well enough that he was only looking out for an opportunity of revenge upon him for having stepped up into his place. All were surprised at seeing the subject of their discourse leave the school-house, after

arranging the forms and desk of his class for
the afternoon school, as he had done nearly
two years ago when promoted from a lower
one, and then walk quietly homewards, totally
regardless of sundry taunting remarks which
must, however, have reached his ears.

Maggie met him at the bottom of the garden steps.

" Well, Hughie ! "

" Well, Maggie ! "

" You know what I mean. Has anything
been found out, and—and—was it very hard?
I've been longing to see you come back ! "

" It's been very hard," replied her brother,
despondingly ; for his thoughts on his homeward walk had, as might have been expected,
been busy with the morning's trials. " I'm
afraid I shan't keep on, though—though—I
think it's right."

" But didn't any one stand up for you ? "

" One of the fellows said he was sure it
wasn't me, and Reynolds said, ' Cheer up, old
boy, you'll come out of it all right.' It was
nice his saying that."

" And Mr. Evans ? "

" Mr. Evans has come only three months

ago, and doesn't know me; and I believe he suspects me."

"He can't; I'm sure he doesn't really!"

"This morning's made me feel different again, Maggie; I thought I'd be strong all at once to get over my disliking that fellow, and I tried in school, but now I feel—"

Hugh left his sister to understand the nature of his feelings by resorting to whistling, which relieved his mind, as by some peculiar connection or construction of our constitution, whistling generally does. Maggie looked very thoughtful.

"I think the only way of getting to feel right will be by doing something good-natured in return for his being provoking—like the Bible says, 'overcoming evil with good.' Because you see, Hugh, if you can't get right about *him*, it'll go into all the rest and spoil it." A rather enigmatical speech of Maggie's, but her brother understood it perfectly.

"I don't know, Maggie, I never felt so little sure about myself; and yet, trying this morning's done me good in a way."

"Don't you remember, Hugh, that picture of Christian in the Pilgrim's Progress going down into the Valley of Humiliation, and how slippery and difficult it is, yet when he got down and walked there, he found it pleasant and easy?　Perhaps it's the beginning that's so hard."

"I thought he met Apollyon there," replied her brother; "I know there's a splendid likeness of him (Apollyon, I mean) just about there, for I painted it myself."

"Well, I believe he did," rejoined Maggie, hesitating; "but Faithful didn't; and don't you remember he frightened Shame away by saying, '*Before honour is humility.*'　There's a text for you, Hugh!"

"It seems to suit just now,—at least I hope it may prove so," he answered.

"It'll be better that it should have happened when father comes home," said Maggie, who saw that her brother needed encouraging; "he'll love you much more for being willing to be low than for climbing up high."

"If I keep on," he replied; "if only I can. Come along in to dinner."

"No, one thing first; I've found out one thing from Jamie."

"About Friday?"

"Yes. You know you thought nobody knew about Mr. Evans's register, because before he came the schoolmaster didn't keep a copy of the marks—only the one Mr. Malcolm kept."

"Well, what of that?"

"Jamie knew. I got it out of him this morning. Somehow he's so close, Jamie is,—not a bit like you and Nannie,—he puzzles me so."

"But how did he find it out?"

"He was in Mr. Evans's house last month for a message, and he was just outside the door when Mrs. Evans was moving the things from the table; and Jamie heard Mr. Evans say, 'Take care of that paper, it's my copy of marks, and I shall have to add it up for the prizes by-and-by.' Then she said, 'I thought you sent them to Mr. Malcolm;' and he said, 'I always keep a copy for myself, so that I needn't trouble Mr. Malcolm when I add up for the examination.' Jamie heard that."

"Did he tell Carson?"

"I can't make out. I tried to make him tell me, and where he was on Friday after school, but he said he was late and must go."

"That's one thing gained," said Hugh,

hopefully ; "you must try again at Jamie,—
you manage him best."

"The worst is that he gets vexed, and then
tells mother I worrit at him ; and really she
thinks so."

"Oh no, she doesn't ; now I'm hungry, let
us go in."

The four brothers and sisters walked together to school that afternoon,—Maggie with
Jamie, whose hand she held though he wanted
to run on before. He was so contradictory
and shuffling in his replies to her questions,
that she did not succeed in gaining much.
But she learnt by skilful questioning that
Jamie had let out his knowledge of the duplicate mark-paper to Carson, and also that he
had been the one to find the missing keys,
which had been restored to Mr. Evans on the
Friday afternoon. He said he had found
them in a corner of a class-room, but would
not help Maggie to guess how they had come
there. She asked how he had found them ?
He replied that it had been his turn to clear
the small class-room before afternoon school,
and that he had come early to do so, and had

found them then. It suddenly occurred to his sister that it was in the waste-paper basket belonging to this very room that the torn mark-paper which Reynolds had thrown aside was found, and that as Jamie had, by his own account, arrived only *just* in time to settle the room before school opened, it must have been in the basket when he went as usual to clear it. She questioned him on this point, but he replied that he had not touched the paper-basket, as it was late, and it often remained uncleared till evening. When asked where he had been between the close of morning school and dinner-time, he looked embarrassed for a moment and answered, "Round by the meadows."

"And you didn't see any one go into the school-room?"

"No, Maggie; how you tease!"

"Didn't you know Hugh was staying in?"

"No. Yes. Not exactly. I knew he had his map to finish."

"Then you weren't in the play-ground after school, and didn't see him cross it to go to Mr. Evans's house?"

"No, I didn't see him cross it."

"And didn't you see Carson at all between schools?"

"Maggie, how you go on! You're such a girl,—it's just like a girl, bothering so."

"Listen, Jamie," replied his sister, "if you know anything about this, and don't say it out, you're lying in God's sight, and he will punish it. And, O Jamie, when you think what a good brother Hugh is, and how unhappy this has made us, and how he had thought of showing father the prize, while now he's in such disgrace, and everybody thinks so badly of him—you couldn't bear—"

But Jamie had burst into a fit of crying. "I'm miserable about it," he sobbed; "I'd rather father wouldn't come home, I've done nothing for him, and—and—and—I don't know what to say," and his voice was most piteous.

But Maggie was quite steadfast. "I shall tell Hugh all I have heard from you, Jamie," she said; "and if you know anything, it'll come out in time, and think how much better it would be to speak now."

But he burst from her, and stifling the sobs which would come, ran before her into school.

Hugh found the afternoon less trying than the morning, and felt "content to take the lowest place." Mr. Malcolm came in, ostensibly to ask Mr. Evans for the address of one of the scholars, but really to see after the boy to whom he had been truly attached. His eye fell upon the serious, quiet face which bent over the last slate in the class, and he was satisfied with what he read there.

"Was Christie here this morning?" he inquired from Mr. Evans, who followed him into the next room.

"Yes, sir; he's been very steady all day."

"I believe he ought to be at the top of the class now," replied Mr. Malcolm; "I don't believe it was he that altered the paper."

"Of course you know him better than I do, sir; but the proof seems so very strong, though I own, I should not have thought it likely. You see, sir, his asking to stay in, and the alteration of his marks on a paper which he expected would be destroyed, and the blue paint, and it's seeming to be for the advantage of no one else—altogether, sir, it's very strong."

"It is—yes, I fear it *is* strong," was the

10

reply in a perplexed tone of voice. "How did he take his place this morning?"

"Without any remark, sir; really, if I might say so, he seemed to take it as if he knew he deserved it, for naturally, he's such a high spirit."

"Poor boy! It may be that he was over-come and feels his sin; but if so, he'd confess it. Good-day, Mr. Evans, I hope he'll be proved innocent yet."

"Good-day, sir." And Mr. Evans closed the door, wondering that a gentleman for whom he had so great a respect should have faith in Hugh, in spite of such clear evidence against him. And yet, when on re-entering the schoolroom, he for a moment observed the subdued, tranquil expression of the boy's face, he absolutely detected the thought so derogatory to the claims of circumstantial evidence stealing clandestinely into his own mind, and found himself inwardly saying, "Can it be that there is some mistake?" Of course the thought was dismissed, but, nevertheless, it returned more than once.

And so more than a month passed away, and the Christies heard that homeward bound ships, more rapid in their transit than the *Heron*, had spoken her on their course, and had reported that so far all was well. The children had made a sort of notched calendar on Robinson Crusoe's principle, which most satisfactorily told the decrease of the number of days at the expiration of which their father's arrival might be expected; and the bundle of letters to be read as had been planned grew sensibly smaller and smaller.

Their feelings respecting his arrival were not so similar as they had been on the day when those plans were laid; on the contrary, with three of the four they were more or less mixed feelings. As far as she herself was concerned, Maggie had no thoughts but joyful ones. Her plan had prospered. Little Ailie was to be transferred in the space of a month to a happy home in the Orphanage. Through Maggie's self-denying efforts she had been able to attend school regularly, thus exchanging the bad examples and neglected manners of Mrs. Carson's house for a scene of happy, healthful occupation. Her gratitude to her friend was unbounded. She hoped she should not be afraid of Mr. Christie, she exclaimed, for fear

she would not be able to tell all that his
Maggie had done for her; and even if she were,
little Alice continued, she would not mind,
for he must hear how happy his Maggie had
made her, when she thought she would never
be happy again.

Nannie's ecstasies as the day drew near,
and she felt that *the* chapter was perfect,
knew no bounds. Her mother, innocent as
she was of the grand designs, had delighted
her beyond description by saying, one day,
that Nannie must get on with her spelling, so
as to be able to please her father with a lesson
in the spelling-book. "Perhaps, in another
year," Mrs. Christie went on to say, "she
might be able to read a chapter." It was a
good thing that she was obliged to look to
the fire at that moment, or Nannie would
have betrayed all. She nodded to Maggie,
signing to her to touch Hugh, who was to
look at Jamie, so that all might appreciate
this delightful remark. She began in a loud
whisper: "If mother only knew," which it
required a frown to the utmost extent of
Maggie's capability to check, while Hugh whispered to her to be quiet, whereupon Mary

Christie looked up, saying, "What is it?" whereupon Nannie said, "Nothing," and began to laugh, and her mother said she couldn't think what had come to the child.

Hugh had worked his way up again in his class, and now stood second only to Carson, who, naturally very clever, and now more than ever determined to keep above his rival, maintained his position. But Hugh did not now feel as he had felt at first; he had begun to gather some of the flowers in the Valley of Humiliation, and found them very fragrant. He felt happier in doing right *for right's sake*, than he had ever felt when working for a prize; and though now and then the thought of his father's disappointment on finding him with such an imputation on his character disturbed him, he could not but feel confident at times that *his* word would be received as the truth, even in spite of appearances.

With respect to Carson himself,—who, especially since Jamie's admissions, he could not but be more and more convinced was the real author of his trouble, though nothing could be proved against him,—he began to entertain different feelings. The sense of his

seeking to work from the highest motives in
one respect, influenced his behaviour in others,
as it always does.   The thought of His words
who had said, " If ye forgive not men their
trespasses, how shall your heavenly Father
forgive you your trespasses ?" had dwelt upon
his mind, and gradually a feeling of pity for
one who he felt must have a weight upon his
conscience, while he was a stranger to the
happiness which Hugh himself had been learning to taste, made him willing to go further
in his new course by endeavouring to overcome evil with good.

The first instance was a trifling one.   Carson was bending over a sum just before
school opened.   " I'd do it in a moment," he
remarked in a vexed tone to one of the other
boys, " if only I had the rule to look at again,
but I can't find my book."   Hugh knew that
if the sum were not ready before the opening,
Carson would lose his place ; and for a moment he triumphed in the thought.   Then
came the new feelings—the new hopes and
determinations to strive for the " overcoming"
which is a greater overcoming than that of
earthly warfare, and quietly taking his own

book, he brought it to Carson with the words, "Here's the place where the rule is, you'll be done in time."

Carson looked up in surprise. "Oh!—thank—thank you," he said, slowly, and as if, while taking time for thinking how he should proceed, he wished to dwell upon words that could not in any sense commit him—"Don't you want it?" But Hugh was gone—gone with a feeling within, which, as Maggie had said, was better than any prize. Carson's manner was very constrained and awkward after this, and still more so when early in the next week, his rival gave up to him his place at cricket, to prevent his being excluded from the game which had begun before he came out. He could not make it out; and, in fact, had the truth been known, would rather that Hugh had adopted any other mode of behaviour towards him. At first he had imagined that it was merely intended to conceal some burst of dislike which would follow, but when constrained to believe that he was mistaken, the uncomfortable conviction forced itself upon his mind, that, in spite of all that had happened, Hugh was treading higher ground than he, and in a path of which he at present knew nothing.

And with Hugh it was well. That promise that "if any man will do his Saviour's will, he shall know of the doctrine whether it is of God," was being fulfilled; and the truth that the shepherd-boy sang, "He that is humble ever shall have God to be his guide," was being made good to him. The path was daily less difficult. The remembrance of his alleged disgrace, though fresh in *his* mind, was becoming fainter in the minds of others. The looking out for opportunities of doing his duty "as unto the Lord," was a source of delight which, though previously frank, joyous, and outwardly well-behaved, Hugh had yet never before experienced. Then Maggie, his own faithful sister, was always at hand to cheer him up and help him on; and though she was a girl, and he was not without the boyish failing of looking down on girls from the fact of their not being raised upon a pedestal of superior physical strength—though she was a girl, he often consciously, but more often unconsciously, deferred to her opinion and judgment, and made her his counsellor.

And so Hugh now looked forward to his father's return with the conscious hope that he was more ready for it—more what that father desired than he had been six months before. And though sometimes failing, he was fighting in earnest as a soldier of the cross—of that cross at which he had learned the lesson of forgiveness and humility.

Jamie was still a puzzle to them all. Though so young, he was naturally cautious and reserved in character, which was the case with none of the rest. He had lost all spirit for joining in any preparations for his father, and it was evident to Hugh and Maggie that he was in Carson's power in some manner of which they knew nothing. Their mother could not think what was over him, and tried to brighten him up with recounting the pleasures which would follow upon his father's return; but these attempts were singularly unsuccessful.

One day, Hugh made him walk alone with him in spite of his evident shrinking from his society, and begged him to confide to him or Maggie everything that was on his mind; but his entreaties were fruitless, and were queru-

lously replied to.   Hugh said that if he were
afraid of being found out by Carson, he would
protect him from any harm; that he was sure
Jamie must know something which would
help to clear up what had happened the
month before, and that for the last time he
begged him to trust him.   But all was of no
use.   Jamie wondered why Hugh should tease
him, wished that he'd let him alone, thought
it very hard that *he* was to be always troubled
about it—in fact, did everything but speak
out, so that Hugh gave him up as hope-
less.

It was on that very evening that as Maggie,
having wished her mother good night, went
up-stairs towards her own room where Nannie
had been fast asleep for more than an hour,
her brother called softly to her from the door
of his little chamber.

"Maggie," he said, "listen to Jamie; he's
talking so in his sleep."

She entered softly.   The moon-light shone
in so clearly that she had no need of a candle
to guide her to the bed-side, where she listened
to the murmurings, sometimes scarcely audible,
that fell from his lips.

"Do let me tell Hugh—I never thought of it's coming to this—I'd never have told you. Yes, father knows it—they'll know it—Hugh'll hate me worse if I don't. No, I didn't see you, but I knew it was you did it. You put the paper in—father, won't you let me come?—it was his fault."

"Hush, Jamie," said Maggie, touching him gently.

"Then they *have* found it out," he exclaimed, jumping up in fear; and then, on seeing his brother and sister, and gradually remembering where he was, he added, "What are you here for?"

"You're talking so, Jamie," replied Maggie; "go to sleep quietly." And she raised the pillow and stood by till he went off again more tranquilly.

The next morning she and Hugh consulted upon what they had heard. "I shall speak to Carson alone," said the latter quietly, "and tell him what Jamie has been saying in his sleep. I shall tell him that we've seen for a long time that there's been something on his mind, and that he's pretty much let it out now. I shall ask him to go to Mr. Malcolm

and acknowledge it himself.   It'll be much
better than waiting for it to come out."

"What can have made him behave so?
And then, how has he bound poor little Jamie
so close?"

"I expect that he's got Jamie into doing
something wrong, and then threatened to tell
father and mother if he didn't do as he
ordered him.   Good-bye, Maggie."

When Hugh arrived at school, Carson was
not there, but Mr. Evans received a note from
his father saying that he had been taken
with something like rheumatic fever after
rowing the evening before, and that he was
very unwell.

Mr. Evans remarked that he was very sorry
that one of the best pupils in the school
should be laid up, especially now that the
holidays were near, but that he hoped that he
would be well in time to receive the tokens of
approbation which his progress deserved. Some
of the boys touched each other significantly at
the close of this somewhat dignified and
formal speech ; one said "that's a good 'un,"
and one or two whispered that master was
"a new hand."   Otherwise, little notice was

then taken of the circumstance, though, after
school, several ran up to Hugh, who was fast
regaining popularity, with the expressed hope
that now he'd beat Carson after all, "Such a
sneak to keep so well with the new master,
too, who thinks he's quite a pattern!"

"I'm going for a walk," said Hugh the
next day, after afternoon dismissal; "tell
mother not to expect me early."

"Which way?" inquired Maggie.

"Out by the copse," replied her brother
laughing, for they knew that when Jamie said
he was going "out by the copse," he meant
that he was bound for the Carsons' cottage.

It was a fine summer's afternoon, and there
was peace everywhere without; peace, too, in
Hugh's heart which he had not known when
he had trod that way with Maggie only a few
weeks before.

Alice Donald ran out to meet him. "Will's
so bad," she said hastily, "and cross—as cross
as aunt herself. The doctor says it's rheumatic fever, and that he'll be down for weeks."

"I've come to see him," said Hugh.

"You! why, when he's so bad to you, why
should you?"

"Hasn't Maggie taught you?" he answered, "Alice, are we only to care for kind people?"

Little Alice coloured. "I see," she replied, " only—"

"Only what?"

"Why—don't be angry—I wasn't sure—I knew Maggie was like that—but—but I didn't know you had come to be so."

" Only trying, Ailie," was the reply as he went in.

Carson looked not a little surprised when his visitor appeared. "What's made you come?" he inquired, tossing painfully on the bed.

"I wanted to know how you were, and here's a book Mr. Evans sent you to read—a nice one it looks."

"Why should you have brought it?"

" Well, one's glad to be neighbourly, you know; besides, I want to talk to you."

"I'm too bad; there's isn't a bone that doesn't ache like anything. I couldn't read anyhow."

" Shall I read a bit to you," said Hugh, trying to forget the game of cricket about to begin on Airie Green; "here's a good story of four sailors on a desert island. I'd like to have been with them for a time."

" Don't mind about staying," growled Carson painfully ; "it'll keep you from the Green ; perhaps I may try and read a bit myself by-and-by."

"Suppose I begin," said Hugh, who saw that Carson, whose active mind needed something to occupy it, wavered between the desire to listen and a half ashamed feeling which made him shy of accepting the proffered service ; "here goes!"

He read for some time, and his auditor, who had not yet said good-bye to that period of boyhood at which every boy longs to be a second Robinson Crusoe, was soon listening intently.

" I must go now," said Hugh at last, laying down the book ; "it's not half a bad book, is it ?"

" No, it's real good ; only, it seems so odd your taking the trouble to come and read to me. Nobody else does ; mother can't, and Alice isn't anything of a reader,—but I can't make you Christies out—any of you."

" I'll come again when I can," replied Hugh ;

"besides, I want to speak to you very much when you're better, but I won't mind now. Good-bye."

This was the first of many visits to Carson, whose illness increased rather than subsided. To listen to reading was one of the few pleasures which he was able to enjoy, and gradually he came to anticipate the hour which Hugh would spend with him with the gratification with which a prisoner confined to a sick-bed looks forward to the welcome event which breaks the weary monotony of the long feverish days and nights.

"How much are you selling your eggs for now?" asked Hugh of Jamie, one morning after breakfast.

"A penny each, the new-laiders," replied the poultry-keeper; "and ninepence a dozen, those for setting."

"Well, I'll buy a new-laid egg every day for a time," rejoined his brother; "here goes for the first;" and he threw a penny high up into the air, which, by a feat of agility, Jamie caught in his hands.

"Who are they for?" he inquired.

"Why shouldn't they be for myself?"

replied Hugh ; "don't you think I'm looking delicate, and want nourishing ?" And with his bonnie open countenance, and rosy cheeks, and elastic step, he certainly looked very like an invalid.

"It doesn't seem like it," replied Jamie ; "here's the egg. The penny'll make our money-box heavier, at all events, and next week we'll have to buy the present for father." For, as previously arranged, the brothers and sisters had been putting aside various small moneys with the intention of making a joint gift to greet the return of Hugh the elder, though, if the truth must be told, Jamie's contributions had been small compared with those of the others.

"Here's something good for getting well," said Hugh, that afternoon, bringing up to Carson's bed-side the dainty new-laid egg which he and Alice had been cooking down stairs; "it was laid fresh this morning; and here's a little bit of toast made out of Maggie's home-made bread, to eat along with it."

Eating, if fever has departed, and there is the least inclination for food, is quite an interesting event, especially when some little

11

dainty morsel is unexpectedly placed before the sick person. So William felt it, while he contrasted the neatness and delicacy with which Hugh and Alice served up the little repast with the coarse, untidy manner of his usual attendance.

"It's very nice," he said, lying down again; "I never liked an egg so much before. Hugh, you're very queer."

"Am I? Well, I suppose every one is some ways."

"You're different from almost every one," continued Carson; "different from what you used to be yourself."

"I wish to be," said Hugh—hesitatingly, though; "that's what I'm trying for, but—oh dear! it's hard enough sometimes."

"I've had lots of time for thinking alone here," said Carson, "and I've been thinking about—by the way, why hasn't Jamie come to see me?"

"Jamie's got something queer over *him* lately; he's very low about something; we think—Maggie and I—that—that—"

"Well, what?"

"That perhaps you could make him easy;

that's to say, that if you'd let him speak out
—haven't you made him promise to keep
quiet about something ? "

"What makes you think so ? "

"We heard him talking in his sleep ; " and
Hugh repeated all that our reader already
knows, adding, moreover, sundry particulars
respecting the change that had of late come
over the boy.

"Well, he may speak out after to-morrow,"
said Carson, after some minutes of evidently
painful thought, and then hurrying his words
as if he wished them to be beyond recall; "let
him come and see me to-morrow evening,
can't he?"

Hugh promised that he should.

"And Mr. Malcolm ; why hasn't he been to
see me?"

"He's been away for a week," replied the
other, "and only came back yesterday ; and
he's had so much sickness to look after at the
other end of the parish."

"Will you go straight now—right away,
and ask him to come to me to-morrow morning, and say I have something particular to
say to him. Tell him I thought once I was

going to die, and it all came before me—
everything about *that*—you know what I
mean—and—and—I must tell him—soon."

"I'll take the message," replied Hugh,
gravely.

Carson lifted himself painfully from his
pillow. "Hugh Christie," he said slowly,
"you've done what I've read about people
doing, but what I never believed any one
would do to me—you've overcome evil with
good. I hated you—I hated you from the
day you got me into disgrace, and when you
seemed to triumph over my being below you;
and I determined I'd revenge. And ever
since, you've been fighting my hatred away.
I wished you to be different; I wished you to
give anger back for anger; I didn't want
you to be—to be what you have been;
but you've done it; and now, I must give
in, and make things right. So tell Mr.
Malcolm quickly."

The next evening Hugh was working busily
with Maggie and Nannie in the front garden.
His jacket was suspended on an apple-bough,
and his straw hat was thrown on the grass

whilst he assisted his sisters in putting in order the little strip of garden, which, besides producing flowers like any ordinary piece of ground, was through their voices to speak a whole multitude of pleasant greetings to the wanderer on his return home. Jamie had gone "out by the copse," and Mrs. Christie was busied within the cottage, where sundry paperings and settings to rights, and hangings up of pictures were in process. There was no cloud over the happiness of the little party, excepting that which the thought of Jamie now and then raised in the minds of the elder ones, though with that even came the hope that now he would be able to acknowledge the errors that had been evidently weighing on his mind, and would be far happier than he had been for months.

Suddenly Hugh heard a voice calling to him from the gate—a pleasant, kindly voice, which was well known to him; and turning round, he saw Mr. Malcolm standing at the foot of the steps, as if he had been watching them for some minutes. Hugh felt for a hat, which he might take off; but having already parted with his, he picked it up and put it on again, by way of signing respect, and seizing his coat, ran down quickly to meet him.

"Hugh, my boy," inquired Mr. Malcolm, "when do you expect your father?"

"We can't tell exactly, sir; we think the vessel might be in in about a week if they had a good passage, and then, there'd be a day or two before he could come up here."

Mr. Malcolm did not speak further for a minute; then he laid his hand kindly on the boy's shoulder, and said,—

"He'll hear that of his boy which will make him happier than any prize; though the prizes will come too."

Then Hugh, getting up his courage, said, "Have you been to Carson, sir?"

"Yes," replied Mr. Malcolm, gravely; "poor fellow, he's very ill, but he'll be better now this is off his conscience. I couldn't have suspected it, though, for a moment; but it's been no evil to you; that's to say, your heavenly Father has turned it into a blessing. Now let me speak to your mother."

Then Mr. Malcolm went into the cottage with Hugh and Maggie, who followed, and told Mrs. Christie all that Carson had acknow ledged; how he had planned revenge on Hugh, and had learned from Jamie about the duplicate register, and had contrived to hide Mr. Evans's keys for a day or two;—and how he had heard the order to Reynolds when he was in the class-room, and Hugh's request for permission to stay in, and the schoolmaster's direction to him to come for the colour box;—and how, finding Jamie outside, he had contrived to send him out of the way, and then, watching secretly for Hugh's short absence from the school-room, had altered the figures, imitating his, and had left a mark of blue paint on the back of the paper, like what he knew to be in Mr. Evans's colour-box, knowing all the time that the marks would be added up for the prize from the other register;—and then of how, having succeeded, he watched to see where Reynolds would throw the rough copy of marks, and from the play-ground (whence everything in the class-room might be observed), saw him tear it up, and throw it into the identical waste-paper basket before mentioned;—and of how he had, by some excuse, prevented Jamie from clearing the basket, with the intention of keeping the

torn pieces until such time as there should be
inquiries set on foot respecting the discrepancy
between the two registers, which he knew
would be separately added up and compared,
when he would have found the torn list in
some obscure corner, and it would have been
very difficult to prove Hugh innocent (while
the circumstances of his having begged to
remain alone in the room would have been all
remembered), and he, Carson, would have been
brought out first, and his rival infallibly dis-
graced.   Which is a summary of a long story
that Mr. Malcolm made plain to Mrs. Christie,
who listened in wonder that any one should
feel so unkindly to her Hugh.   And then
he told, in many more words than we need
to transcribe, how her boy had quietly taken
the lowest place, and had done his duty
in it; and of how he had been trying to
overcome evil with good, and had won the
victory, and had set an example in the school
which might be of endless advantage.   And
then, Mr. Malcolm went on to say, how different this strife had been from any struggle
for an earthly prize, and much more besides,
until Mrs. Christie seemed inclined to cancel

the flood of tears she had shed on hearing of Hugh's accusation, with another which was to be for joy and pride.

So Mr. Malcolm rose to depart. But Hugh, who had been looking from his mother to Maggie, and from Maggie again to his mother, stopped him for a minute.

"Please, sir," he began, "I shouldn't have gone back to school, and I'm sure I shouldn't have tried to care for Carson, if it hadn't been for Maggie."

His friend looked at the bright, open face of the brother, and then to Maggie's sweet changeful countenance, on which the smiles and the tears had seemed to be playing at hide-and-seek with each other, and, pausing for a minute, he spoke to them of the preciousness of the tie which bound them to each other, and bade them hold fast by each other more and more, and walk hand and hand together through life, and left them with a prayer that the blessing might be upon them that maketh rich and bringeth no sorrow with it.

Then, when Jamie came back there was another story, and a sad one. All his troubles were explained. He had been enticed away

from Hugh into Carson's set, and then he had
felt flattered by their making out that he was
a big boy.   And then, when he got into diffi-
culties with his sums—and arithmetic was
Jamie's grand source of trouble—Carson had
offered to help him and had done the sums
for him.   And then he had tempted him to
play at marbles for money against his parents'
strict commands, which accounted for the dis-
appearance of many a penny originally destined for the joint fund.   And so poor little
Jamie had been alternately flattered, tempted,
and bullied,—had felt no longer any spirit for
the preparations for his father's return ; and
when, having guessed the part Carson had
performed in the alteration of the marks, he
had charged him with it, the latter threatened
to expose all his own wrong-doings which had
gone before if he ever breathed a suspicion of
such a thing into any one's ear.   So poor,
foolish little Jamie, who might have found so
much comfort in confessing everything to his
mother or to his sister, went on miserably day
by day, depending on help dishonestly given for
maintaining his position in the school, and
with the misery daily present to him of see-

ing Hugh suffering, without permission or courage to communicate the suspicions he entertained and the evidence he could have furnished in his favour; suffering, in fact, all the distress which a weak mind experiences when in the power of a strong and a bad one, and when conscience is still alive and doing her work.

It was a long, sad story, told with many tears, and the mother's heart was sore for the trial and trouble that had been paling her boy's cheeks and checking all his happiness for so many weeks. Though he generally thought himself too much of a man to sit on her knee, now he rested his head wearily on her bosom, sobbing out his troubles and his fears that his father would never forgive him. Poor Jamie! he had been early learning the sad lesson that "the way of transgressors is hard."

He was happier now, however, that all the confessions were over, and that Hugh had told him that he would stand by him, and that he was always to trust him, and though the thought that "father was coming home," which was the animating and pervading sub-

ject of all the family discourse, brought a feeling not wholly unmixed with care to his heart,
still the weight of concealment was off his
mind, and his mother assured him that the
dear loving father who was returning would
love him all the same, now that he was forgiven; and the little tired tearful boy knelt
by his bed-side and told his Father in heaven
how he had erred and strayed from his ways
like a lost sheep, and begged him, for Jesus
Christ's sake, to pardon all his sins.   And his
sleep was more peaceful and tranquil than he
he had known for many a night, though his
dreams could hardly have been so bright as
those of the happy brother by his side.

VII.

𝕱ather's 𝕮ome!

" But now you've come at last
  And never more to roam;
O Willie, we have missed you,
  Welcome, welcome home!"

VII.

Father's Come!

IT was the longest day in the year, and, indeed, it seemed the longest to the Christie family, especially to the children, who had risen at some unheard-of hour in the morning in order the sooner to meet all the happiness that it was to bring with it. For a letter had come from Hugh the elder, for which old Duncan had pretended to charge Maggie double postage, declaring that such good tidings ought not to come through the post for a single stamp,—a letter on good, thick, English paper, with an English postmark, but inscribed with the same handwriting which for so many years had directed their Indian letters to Airie, and bearing the joyful intelligence that the *Heron* had safely arrived in port, that, owing to some delay in the delivery of the soldiers' baggage, the writer himself would not, for two days, be able to follow his home-bound missive, but that, at the expiration of that time, he hoped once more to be treading the path across the field which led to the bridge over Airie brook, and to be *at home !*   Maggie told Duncan that he was quite wrong, and that he should have no extra payment as these were anything but heavy tidings ; and then she went to the bank where the red strawberries gleamed from under their dark leaves, and gathered a supply of the ripe fruit for the kind old man, whose eye glistened as he thought of the happiness that was coming to her so soon, and, it might be, of his own cheerless home, where neither wife nor child would ever again be looking out for him.

And this 21st of June was to bring Hugh Christie home. As we have said, the children were up at an unprecedentedly early hour of the morning; in fact Nannie had declared the night before that she thought, upon this one occasion she would like to give up the little ceremony of going to bed altogether, which declaration she carried out by falling fast asleep over a garland at which she was assisting, whereupon her mother carried her up stairs in her arms, and speedily deposited her for the night in her own little dormitory where she was aroused in the gray morning by Maggie's voice sounding in her ears with the words, "Nannie, Nannie, wake up! it's to-day father's coming home!"

Before breakfast, manifold preparations were to be made of a most important nature. In the first place, the decorations of the rooms required completion. A sparkling "Welcome!" in many coloured flowers, hung over the door-way, constructed on an entirely new principle by Hugh and Nannie, the latter having been transported with delight at her elder brother's consenting to take her as partner into the concern. It never occurred to any of the four children that any one but their father could appropriate the welcome, or that a single passer-by could be ignorant of the cause of these rather unusual demonstrations when he looked up to the cottage door. They had the childlike belief that all must know of and rejoice in their joy.

Within, there were bright flowers which

Maggie had distributed in every available direction,—roses, and sweet peas, and carnations, the brothers and sisters of flower-families in the garden outside, who were all to speak the same words of welcome which for many long months they had been trained to speak. And when these were all freshly arranged, Maggie produced out of her secret drawer— the same drawer which contained the precious bundle of letters—a little piece of her own handicraft, which had been so privately executed that not even Hugh had known of its existence. Worked upon a bordered card (the prettiest Mrs. Scott's shop could produce), were the words, " *O give thanks unto the Lord, for he is good; for his mercy endureth for ever,*" and this, when no one was present, Maggie hung up where all would see it; and around it were heart's-ease which had grown in her own garden, and which were chosen to wreath round the word of thanksgiving for reasons good and best known to herself. For in Maggie's heart there was a deeper feeling than gladness, now that the long-expected day had really arrived; or perhaps we should say that her gladness was of a deeper, more earnest kind than that of her brothers and sister. To her there had always been an association of ideas between the thought of the heavenly Father whom not having seen she loved, and the unknown earthly father whom he was restoring to them; a dim, shadowy expectation of finding in one whose name had been dear to her from her cradle, a fond, true friend whose love would, better than any earthly love, show her the meaning of words such as she had often pondered over, with the longing desire more fully to comprehend them, and which tell us that *"like as a father pitieth his children, so the Lord pitieth them that fear him;"* and that *"we have received the adoption of sons whereby we cry, Abba, Father."* Yes, heart's-ease was in Maggie's heart, and great, great thankfulness to him who had heard her prayer and had brought them this joyful day; and when all the preparations were ended, when every weed that had the effrontery to show itself in the front garden since the previous evening had been mercilessly pulled up, and when the children had satisfied themselves that nothing more could be done by way of improvement

in any corner of the house, she half-shyly
whispered the proposition to Hugh that they
should read a few verses together and try to
remember the Giver of all good things in this
day of gladness, Hugh said he could not
read that morning, but that he would rather
sing ; and so they all went together under
the apple tree, and Maggie with her sweet,
clear voice began one of their school hymns:—

> " What shall we render
> Thou heavenly Friend, to thee,
> For love so tender,
> For grace so free!"

Then their mother came out to them, having
been occupied with arrangements in her own
room until then, and the children thought she
had never looked so nice as in the neat new
dress which had been solemnly prepared for
this day, and which was adorned with a bright
ribbon that kind Mrs. Scott had insisted on
furnishing.

The breakfast was rather a tumultuous one,
—indeed it seemed to the children that breakfast was altogether too common-place an affair
to be regarded upon such a day. However, it
was well that the proceedings of the family
should be discussed in full committee, and

Mary Christie was glad to enforce the clearance of sundry substantial slices of bread and butter, declaring that it was all very well to talk, but she never heard that pleasure was to keep folks from starving.

They were none of them clear as to the time when Hugh the elder was to arrive, but it could not be until late in the evening, Mr. Malcolm said, whom Mary had consulted on the subject. Descending from railway dignity, the traveller would have to join a coach at a station about twelve miles from the cross roads, where the way to Airie turned off from the main road. And there at a distance of a mile and a half from his own home, his wife and children had determined to meet him in the evening, which would have seemed a long way off to the young ones, had there not been so many other things to occupy their minds.

For on this morning, it so happened that the school closed, and the prizes were to be given. And so, soon after breakfast, the whole party started for the schoolrooms, which were filled by children and parents, and were, moreover, decorated with so many flowers, that it was a wonder that the Airie gardens should have stood such a tax on their resources.

Maggie was not anxious for herself, but chiefly for her brothers. She had been unable to attend school with regularity on account of her manifold home duties, and so had no thought of a prize. And besides, everything but the great happiness that was coming so soon seemed just then to find little room in her thoughts, and she felt as if in a confused dream while she sat amongst the ranks of her school-fellows, until roused by hearing Mr. Malcolm's voice as it called her brother's name. And then she looked wistfully at Hugh as he came forward with his brave, truthful face, and yet with his head a little lowered as if he would have concealed the burning flush which came to his cheeks. And the flush came more burning still when Mr. Malcolm spoke of what had happened months ago, and of how Hugh had been willing to take the lowest place, and to do his duty in it when he knew himself to be clear of the charge brought against him, through another's sin. And then Mr. Malcolm said something about

his father's coming home to find that his boy
had learnt the lesson which a soldier's son
should learn, because it is one that every true
soldier of Jesus Christ must learn, that God
giveth grace unto the humble ; and he told
Hugh as he gave him a large and handsomely
bound copy of the " Pilgrim's Progress," that
it was always to be a reminder to him that
" before honour is humility." Hugh's " Thank
you, sir," was a very nervous and shy one,
and Maggie felt a longing desire to go up to
him with a loving, " O Hughie, I'm so glad,"
but as this was out of the question, she only
looked it all to him across the room, and then
glanced towards her mother, who was very
much inclined to cry indeed ; and who in her
turn was nodded at, and smiled at, and looked
at benignantly by all the kindly eyes of all
the good mothers around her.

Jamie was only too thankful that his name
was not mentioned. Poor boy! he knew that
there would be no encouraging word for him,
no token of approbation which he might show
to his father. His only hope was that when he
said " how very, very sorry he was," his father
would forgive him, and try to love him still.

The prizes and the good advice which accompanied each one—much in the same way that salt accompanies slices of bread and butter—were long in being distributed. Nannie was overwhelmed with delight at receiving a Testament with gilt edges as a reward for her great improvement in reading, and was still more delighted when Mr. Malcolm said he hoped she would soon have learnt to read in it. Much perplexed in spirit was little Nannie, nevertheless, being very anxious to confide to some one that she could read *one* chapter already, and yet fearful of betraying her secret before her mother. However, prudence, and a vehement pulling at her dress from Jamie who was near her, decided her into being silent, and in a few minutes perfect contentment had resumed its possession of her round, happy features.

Alice Donald was not passed unnoticed. Mr. Malcolm gave her a well stocked work box as a farewell gift from the school on her entering her new home. He made no mention of the little work woman who had befriended her, for it would have distressed that same little lassie in no small degree had he done so.

But Alice could not be silent. "It's all Maggie, sir," was her reply to his kind words, and Maggie's cheeks were hot and tingling in their turn, and became still more so when Mr. Malcolm called her name, and she unexpectedly found herself in front of the assembly, which in her eyes was a very imposing one. There was no school prize for Margaret Christie, he said, as she had not been able to attend with regularity, but he had been commissioned by her companions—especially the younger ones amongst them—to give a beautiful prayer book to her who had won a name which was earned by something better than head knowledge; for this book was destined, Mr. Malcolm said, for "the little children's friend." Whereupon he put the book into the hands of Alice and of little Nannie, who placed it in Maggie's, the latter being unable to restrain the exclamation, "I've known it for a whole week, and never told," whereby were accounted for mysterious looks and nods on Nannie's part which Maggie had puzzled over, and dark and vague hints of something coming which she had hardly had time to notice, but which were fully explained when several little voices murmured as she resumed her seat, "It's with our love, Maggie; and mine —and mine—and mine," until Maggie very nearly cried outright, and was in no small measure relieved when the assembly broke up.

Then came the buzz of congratulations outside, and examinations of presents and prizes; and Mrs. Christie was shaken hands with by friendly neighbours, and finally by Mr. Malcolm himself, who said that *her* prize would come in the evening, which little remark— not so very brilliant after all—was quickly handed about amongst her friends, and was considered as very pleasantly facetious indeed.

Many hours of the day had flown past by the time the family returned home. In three hours more, Mary Christie said, as they rose from a speedily despatched dinner, the children might begin to prepare for their walk to Airie cross, as the place was called where met the four roads above mentioned; and involuntarily five pair of eyes glanced towards the clock, which, with its measured tick, tick, seemed like one of those provokingly calm and

sensible people, who wish it to be understood
that whatever may happen to disturb the
composure of minds less equally balanced,
theirs are far too well regulated to be
liable to unnecessary perturbation or excitement.

"Nearly three o'clock!" exclaimed Hugh.
"Maggie, we'll clear the room and write in
father's Bible. I've brought a new pen from
school on purpose."

Many had been the cogitations respecting
the joint present which Hugh the elder was
to find awaiting him on his return. Hugh
the second had been appointed treasurer, and
had watched over the money box like a miser.
Many small sums had found their way into it
since the plan had been made. He had earned
a little by working for Mr. Malcolm, and by
selling some of his pigeons; and Maggie's bees
had supplied honey which had brought in a
very good return to their owner, and Jamie's
hens had laid well, and it was some comfort
to the little boy, who had his own trouble still
concealed in a corner of his heart, to feel that
latterly, at all events, he had been able to add
a very good proportion to the fund. Nannie's

chief source of emolument had been her little
garden, from which she had made up various
and sundry small nosegays, which she had
brought round to her friends, who, though
they might have gathered much choicer flowers
from their own flower-beds, were by no means
disinclined to buy from the little bouquet
seller, who, when asked what she was to be
paid, replied half shyly, " I can't say, indeed ;
it's for our present to father when he comes."
So Mrs. Malcolm gave Nannie sixpence for
two nosegays, and the schoolmistress gave her
threepence for another, and kind little Mrs.
Scott, whose liberality in the comfit and sugar
candy line made her a favourite amongst all
the juveniles of Airie, insisted on presenting
the little flower woman with the brightest
fourpenny piece in the till, as purchase money
for the last nosegay in her basket, although it
was not at all a pretty one, having been constructed by Jamie of marigolds, sweet-william,
and some rather elderly damask roses.

It had been no easy matter to determine as
to what the present should be, but the question was settled by Mrs. Christie's assurance
that a good-sized, well-bound family Bible

would be most acceptable to the children's father, who had never ceased regretting the loss of his own large Bible which had disappeared for ever on the voyage out to India. And so it was settled. The great business of the inscription had further occupied their thoughts considerably. Hugh was rather anxious that it should be intrusted to Mr. Evans who had a gift for executing miraculous performances with a steel pen, one of which on the opening page of the school register, and representing a swan in full sail from whose tail there proceeded a garland of flourishes which encircled the page and resulted with surprising precision in the first elaborate letter of the inscription of the title had been an object of admiration and emulation to all the school boys of Airie. But Maggie thought her father would rather have their own writing to meet his eye whenever he opened his Bible; and Mrs. Christie thought so too, and Jamie and Nannie, who in school were still " on slates" and not even " in copy-books," were much pleased at the prospect of writing their names, although, when the ceremony came to be performed,

Nannie had to yield her hand to her brother's guidance as the little fat round fingers were not yet in sufficient training to form the letters by themselves.

They all looked with great satisfaction at the completed inscription which Hugh, in whose best handwriting it was executed, read aloud:—

This Bible is given to our dear Father, on his coming home to us from abroad, by his affectionate Children.

> *Hugh Ernest Christie.*
> *Margaret Christie.*
> *James Christie.*
> *Ann Mary Christie.*

Then the Bible was closed and placed in the centre of the table, and the morning's presents and prizes were arranged in order around it, and the children looked about for something to do which might occupy them during the weary two hours of waiting.

" Let us read father's last letter over again," said Jamie, " that'll take us some time at all events."

" And let us all sit down and settle once

more what he'll be like," said Nannie; "just once more before he comes."

"We've settled over and over," said Hugh. "I think it'd be better fun to climb or run about; I can't keep still."

"It's very hot, Hugh," said Maggie, "and we'll have the walk by-and-by. Suppose we do, as Jamie said, and read the letter again; it'll be like finishing up with the bundle we began six long months ago."

Hugh was in his very most amiable of moods, and assented. Possibly he, too, might have owned to feeling a little bit tired after all the morning's proceedings; and unowned to each other, there was a half shy and timid feeling creeping amongst the children as the evening came on which made them glad to be together, while their mother told them to be quiet down stairs as she was busy in her own room above.

It was a hot, drowsy afternoon, cooler indoors than without; and Maggie opened the front door which looked out over Airie, and the back door opposite which opened upon the little well-kept garden, and which was overshadowed by the apple tree wherein many and many a consultation had been held by the brothers and sisters in parliament assembled, and seating herself in its shade with her work in her hand, she was followed thither by Hugh, who established himself on one of the lower boughs with the letter which he had obtained from his mother, and by Jamie and Nannie, who busied themselves with plaiting some of the long grass into different twists and shapes.

Their brother began:—

"MY DEAREST WIFE AND CHILDREN,

"This comes to tell you that through God's mercy I have reached England safely, after a prosperous voyage. I was so delighted to see the old white cliffs again, and to think that in a few days more I should be with you all. I cannot get at my baggage, and there has been some delay about the soldiers' things which makes me fear that I shall be two or three days still without seeing you; but you may be sure I shall be as quick as possible, and that the time will seem long till I get to Airie.

"I can hardly fancy so much happiness as being with you again, and I am trying every hour to think whether my dear Mary will be changed, and what all my dear children have grown to be. I often wonder whether they long to see me again as much as I do to see them. I am almost too happy to write to you, and feel so impatient to see you that I cannot sit still any longer. So no more this time from your affectionate husband and father,

"HUGH CHRISTIE."

"It seems too happy to be real," said Maggie; "think of this being the last of our talks and readings that we began on the beach in the winter that day when the letter came."

"Yes, our planning day," exclaimed Nannie; "and there were to be so many things for us to become—that's to say—I mean—you know, Maggie, humble and gentle, and kind to each other, and truthful. Oh dear! I'm afraid he'll not like me after all."

"Yes he will," said Jamie. "I think you're much nicer than you used to be."

"You only say so because I made the tail for your kite all that afternoon," said Nannie; "but father won't know of that."

"He will know that you have been trying hard to please him," said Maggie; "and Jamie's quite right. Jamie's been trying, too, lately."

Poor Jamie was very conscious of the meaning of Maggie's "lately," and was silent for a minute or two. Hugh was the next to speak.

"I believe Maggie's most like what father intends of us all," he said. "Any of us would have got tired long before of working for Alice Donald, and —"

He was interrupted by the appearance of

13

his mother, who, having finished all preparations, had come to join her children. She stood in the shade of the house, looking down with happy eyes upon them, and Maggie thought that no mother in Airie looked so nice as did Mary Christie with her pleasant, kind face and honest smile, especially as she had come down in the neat new cap with white ribbons which she had been making up for this happy day, and which well suited the dark hair folded back from her brow quite plainly, and, as Hugh said, "without any nonsense."

"Come, mother, talk about father," said Nannie, jumping up and drawing her mother's arm round her, "it seems a long time to six o'clock still."

Her mother did not answer, for her eye had fallen on Maggie's face in which a sudden rush of red had been succeeded by a still more sudden paleness. Alone of all the party, she faced the door opposite to which they were assembled, and she alone was so situated as to observe what passed without in the front garden.

"Maggie, child, what's the matter?" inquired her mother.

Maggie did not reply, for a shadow had fallen across the threshold, and a footstep was heard on the gravel walk without, and Mary Christie had turned round in sudden haste and surprise, and her eyes met those of one standing at the door whose face was no stranger face, but whose memory had followed her through long years of waiting and separation, and with a cry of "Hugh! *my* Hugh!" she was in her husband's arms.

With all their privileges, story-tellers have no right to make public to the world certain home scenes which ought to be sacred from intrusion of any curious gaze, and we will for one short half hour leave the inhabitants of Airie cottage to themselves, not even listening without to hear the exclamation, "And this is my Maggie!" "and Hugh!" "And these are my little ones!" nor pausing to explain how the impatient father had contrived to take advantage of a light gig which brought him much sooner to the cross roads than the lumbering coach would have done that did not start from the station for more than an hour after the arrival of the train; and how he had looked up to the old house with longing, lov-

ing eyes to see the "welcome" with which
the children had greeted him, and how—

No, we will not go further.   As we said
before, for half an hour, kind reader, we shall
leave the Christie family in their home, only
as we close the door, catching the sound of
Hugh's exclamation, " It's he!   Father's come
home at last!"

VIII.

Heart's-ease Gathering.

"There's no place like home!"

VIII.

Heart's-ease Gathering.

IT seemed all too good to be true; and yet—it was true. Mary Christie knew that it was true when she sat once more in the old place by her husband's side, as in years gone by, whilst the weary interval of separation seemed to have been a long, vivid dream, so little was the well-remembered face aged or altered. And Maggie knew that it was true, when the gaze of her father's dark eye, met that of her blue, wistful ones, and when she felt his hand resting upon her head, as he said, "My Maggie." And Hugh knew that it was true, when, with a half-proud glance at his first born son, his father said something about his having been a comfort to his mother and sisters, which the boy did not, however, clearly make out, as it had never occurred to him

that he was more so than other boys of his age, though every one else knew that he was. And Jamie and Nannie knew that it was true, when, after a time, their father took them up, one on each knee, and promised to tell them long stories of lions and tigers, and to represent a tiger for Nannie's benefit, at the very first opportunity; so that they were not in the least shy with him, and confided their opinions to each other, when, afterwards in the garden, where all four had after a time withdrawn to leave their parents together, that father was much better than even they had expected; while Hugh and Maggie stood leaning against the apple-tree, hardly knowing how to realize that the moment to which, ever since they could remember, they had looked forward as that which was to be the brightest of their lives, had really come and gone.

They gathered round him, when, after what seemed to them a long interval, he joined them, leaving his wife within; she being now intent on providing a repast which should be suitable for the occasion, and concerning which she and Maggie had held manifold consultations that had resulted in very visible and satisfactory results. Hugh Christie the elder, with his tall, soldier-like bearing, and with the kindly smile upon his face, was a father to be proud of. Nannie would have had him at once look at the garden and the flower-beds, and at sundry out-door preparations for his reception; but Maggie gently whispered, "Not now," and she was silent. Her father cared more to look at his own home-flowers than at any others, however fair. It was the thought of this meeting which had cheered him through long years of soldier life; it was this prospect which had brightened weary hours of fatigue and exhaustion; these were the dear child faces which he had pictured to himself in his daily and hourly imaginings and which had appeared to him in his dreams of home and fatherland.

"We thought to-day would never come," whispered Maggie, half shyly, as she felt his hand stroking the fair hair off her forehead.

"We made a calendar," said Hugh, "when your letter came in the winter; and we notched off every day, and last night it came to the last time, and we all looked at it together, and could hardly think it was really come to the end."

His father's eye was upon his boy now with a fond, happy gaze, and then little Nannie put in for her share of notice. "Yes, we've all been trying, and we made such plans down that day by the beach ; but Hugh and Maggie have done most, only they're so much older—and we joined together, and—oh, I forgot, I mustn't tell, but O father, you'll be so glad when we show you—why do you look so, Jamie? I'm not going to say anything!" Whereupon, Nannie suddenly found herself elevated in her father's arms to a very considerable altitude, whilst Maggie ran into the house to her mother's assistance.

There was a tremble in his voice, as, with folded hands the children stood round the table, and, by Mary's side, he began to return thanks for the undeserved mercies sent from their heavenly Father. And, when his eye rested on Maggie's text, hung opposite to him, he took the words into his own lips, as the heart's-ease was in his heart, and said solemnly, "We give thanks unto thee, O Lord, for thou art good; for thy mercy endureth for ever; through Jesus Christ our Lord."

And now, though it would be much more in accordance with all one's notions and ideas concerning such an occasion, were we to record that "plentiful as was the fare with which the table was spread, the hearts of those who surrounded it, were too full to allow of their doing much in the way of participation," yet our veracity will by no means allow of such a statement. On the contrary, it may fairly be admitted, that the preparations made by Maggie and her mother were most fully appreciated by every one of the party. Her father owned to regarding them with additional satisfaction, when he knew that the light bread had been baked by his Maggie, and that the radishes were from Jamie's garden; and, when he knew that Nannie had supplied the flowers with which she had insisted on adorning the cake, and that the fresh butter had been made by his neat-handed wife, in the same old-fashioned churn which had been his mother's, and which had remained in the house ever since he was a boy. Then, when a bee buzzed through the win-

dow, and hummed inquiringly about the room,
Nannie declared that it had come on a message from the hive to know how father liked
the honey, whilst Hugh, with some pride, un-
covered the basket of fresh fruit, which was in
great part the return of his labours in the
back garden, and divided out the ripe strawberries amongst the party. There was, indeed, joy and gladness in the Airie home that
evening, and the sunset-light streamed through
the open window, and lit up the bright faces
which told so plainly of sunshine within,
whilst every one felt a difficulty incident to
re-unions after long absence, of having so
much to say, as to be uncertain how to begin.

Airie looked still, and calm, and bright,
when later on, parents and children stood without in the garden, while Hugh Christie sur-
veyed the well-remembered landscape, and
observed how the trees had grown up round
the church, and how familiarly the old woods
seemed to rustle out a welcome, when re-
minded to that effect by the evening breeze
which came up from the sea, and how un-
changed was the appearance of the brook-side
walk, where he and his Mary had strolled

together in the long summer evenings when
she was Mary Innes still.   Even the children,
whose joy had been tumultuous a little while
before, were sobered unconsciously by the in-
fluences of the quiet without, and of the deep
gladness within.   And, whilst they stood
there, the silence was broken by the far-off
sound of a flageolet, upon which some unseen
player was solacing himself at the close of the
day's busy occupations ; and, as if he had
known who were listening in the distance, he
let forth the sweet tones of "Home, sweet
home," which sounded as a welcome from
Airie to the returned soldier, who looked
round upon his wife and children with the
heart-felt words, "There's no place like home."

And so night came at last, and "the plans"
had not been spoken of, as the elder ones
agreed that "it would be much better to-
morrow."   But the garden had been already
admired to their full contentment by their
father, as had been also the preparations
within the cottage ; and when they went in,
and the Bible which was their joint present
was placed in his hands by Jamie, whom the
others agreed should have the pleasure of

giving it, they were more than satisfied with the
reception that it received. With a glistening
eye, Hugh the elder read the names on the
fly-leaf, and assured his children that no
greeting could have been so welcome ; and he
showed them a little worn-out Bible which
had been with him through all his marches,
and of which the print was, he said, far too
small for his eyes, which were growing old.
Whereupon, as might have been expected, there
arose an outcry, to the effect that he was not
old by any means, and that he was a dearer
(from Maggie), nicer (from Nannie), jollier
(from Hugh and Jamie), father than they
could under any circumstances have anticipated.
And then the old clock sounded, and Mrs.
Christie looked at Nannie, with the expression
of countenance which, in maternal physiogno-
mies, precedes a suggestion of bed, whereupon
Nannie became inexpressibly fidgetty and disturbed in mind, until, to her great delight, the
very words which she had anticipated, fell
from her father's lips,—

"My dear, shouldn't we have a chapter all
together?"

"Of course we will," replied his wife, while

Nannie made faces at Jamie, to try and prevent him from laughing as her prophecies were fulfilled ; Hugh shall read it."

Hugh was leaning out of the window and did not hear his name mentioned ; and Nannie looked unutterable anxiety at the back of his head.

"Come in, Hugh," said his mother, laying her hand upon his shoulder ; "come in and read a chapter before the little ones go up stairs."

Hugh obeyed, and half mechanically took up the Bible, quite unconscious that Nannie's eyes, full of reminder, were fixed upon him. He was just beginning with a forgetfulness absolutely unpardonable to inquire, "Where shall I read?" when the words "O Hugh!" pronounced in a tone of reminder, of surprise, and of subdued indignation fell upon his ear, and with a sudden coming to himself, he said, "Let Nannie read, father."

"Nannie!" repeated both parents together ; while his mother added, "Nannie doesn't know how to spell through the spelling-book yet."

Never did heart of competitor for academic

honours beat more nervously than did Nannie's
at that moment, while the little scene was in
course of being enacted which she had for so
long anticipated.

"I'll try," she interposed, as her father raised
her upon his knee; and drawing the Bible—his
new Bible—towards her, she began to read in
timid, childlike voice of the Good Shepherd
who giveth his life for the sheep. If she could
have looked up into the kind face above hers,
she would have known that she had not tried
so hard in vain. No music had ever sounded
so sweetly in Hugh Christie's ears as did the
soft voice of the little one on his knee as she
read slowly and reverently the promises which
had often been to him as cold waters in a
thirsty land. And when, having finished,
Nannie closed the Bible and looked up half
shyly and half triumphantly, there was that in
her father's good-night kiss, which more than
told her how well she had succeeded.

Her mother seemed the most surprised, however. "It passes me entirely," she exclaimed;
"why, I thought the child couldn't spell yet,
and she's been reading like the parish-clerk
himself. The school-missus shall hear of this.

Why Nannie, you never told me how you'd been getting to be such a scholar."

"It was a secret, mother," exclaimed the little maiden elated with her success; "it was my plan —Hugh and Maggie advised me, and helped me—it was for father's coming home—I wanted so much to have a plan too." Whereupon followed many more pleasant words and admiring remarks from both father and mother, so that Nannie departed more than satisfied with the result of her undertaking, and with her arms round Maggie's neck as the latter deposited her in her bed exclaimed, before falling to sleep, "O Maggie, it's better than ever we thought, having father home again!"

They neither of them knew that when sleep had visited them that night, there bent over them the forms of their father and mother who, shading away the light, gazed with loving eyes upon the sisters as they lay so still, locked in deep repose. There was a smile upon Maggie's lips of perfect happiness, a smile which told that even in her dreams the newly realized joy was present with her, and filled her mind. And Hugh Christie, the strong, brave soldier, who in distant lands had dreamt of the little

14

ones at home, and had scarcely dared hope that all his visions of returning to them would become one day real and true, gathered from Maggie's smile another blossom of the heart's-ease which he had found planted in his Airie home; heart's-ease which his wife's observations, as they closed the door, to the effect that the other children were all very well, but Maggie, she always knew, was too good for this world, did not in any degree take away.   Every mother settles that one of her children is " too good to live," which prophecy, however, has fortunately not always been found practically to affect its continuance here below.

IX.

Conclusion.

"Jesus said, I will come again and receive you unto myself."

IX.

Conclusion.

MANY were the greetings of the next day. Friends who had known Hugh Christie as a lad, now came to recall the old times of companionship; and many whom he had never known came with kindly congratulations to his wife and children. Old Duncan came with his halting gait and cheery smile to look on the lad, as he still called the manly, middle-aged soldier, for whom he had once strung bows, and constructed arrows by the brook side. And pleasant little Mrs. Scott came to say how really she was so very glad nobody knew; and how she had said to Scott the night before, "Now really, Scott, it does seem so pleasant like to think of that poor thing that's waited so long having her husband, and those dear children having their father back,

that I don't know how to think of anything
else;" and how Scott had replied that it was quite
impossible to say how gratified he felt when
he considered of it ; and how she had determined to come up to the cottage the very next
morning to discharge all the congratulations
which weighed upon her mind, and which resulted in a fervent embrace of Maggie, and a
vehement shaking of hands with her father, and
the donation of a cream-cheese to Mrs. Christie,
which she declared she had made up her mind
to give whenever her husband should return,
and which was placed upon the table and par-
taken of with bread by friendly visitors very
much in the manner of wedding-cake and wine
in more genteel circles, a resemblance not so
very inappropriate after all, as Mary Christie
said it almost seemed like being married over
again to have her husband back after such a long
time, only that she was happier now than even
before.   Later on in the day, arrived Mr. Malcolm, who said that his having known Mrs.
Christie and her children for so long made him
anxious to form acquaintance with her husband.   Whereupon followed a series of gratified courtesies from the former, and a military

salute from the individual addressed, who thanked his visitor for his kindness to his wife and family, not in set well-turned phrases, but with a grateful expression of his feelings which came straight from the heart, and which was real and genuine as was everything else about him. And then, after a time, Mr. Malcolm began to speak of Hugh and Maggie, and said many things concerning them which it gladdened their father's heart to hear, while sensible Mrs. Christie agreed with herself that it was just as well that they were out in the garden all the while, for Mr. Malcolm told all the story of Carson, and of Hugh's conquest over himself, and of his having taken the lowest place when he knew that he had been wrongly judged, and all that our readers know already, while Hugh the elder, could only exclaim at intervals, "The boy was right, sir, the boy was right," remarking at the conclusion, "I'd rather hear that of my lad, sir, than that he was the first scholar in the land."

And so it happened that with Mr. Malcolm's visit began the disclosure of the various undertakings which the brothers and sisters had planned for their father's return, Nannie's only having been revealed the evening before. Alice Donald came in quest of Maggie early in the afternoon, and in her new dress which proclaimed her adoption into the orphan home, and with her grateful love to the friend who had so untiringly helped her on through her troubles, she told to Maggie's father a story of his child's humble endeavour to carry out his desire for her that she should "look on the things of others," which filled him with thankfulness. And then the prizes were produced, and the relation made by Hugh of the day when his father's letter arrived, announcing his intended return, and of the plans made on the beach ; and of how his letters had been their guide in telling them what he would like them to do, and of how they had read the same letters every week until he came, and had been afraid that he would expect them all to be much better than they were, which narration was interrupted by short explanatory notes from Maggie, and by longer ones from Nannie the reverse of explanatory, but which, nevertheless, her father liked to hear, although her brother declared that she mixed everything together in a manner entirely unjustifiable. Jamie's story was told afterwards when he and his mother were alone with his father—a sorrowful story of disobedience, and deceit, and carelessness, which seemed all the more sorrowful when contrasted with Hugh's relation which had gone before. But he felt much relieved when all had been told; and when Mrs. Christie said how very, very sorry her boy had been, and when he heard his father's voice kindly comforting him and saying that he was quite sure now that Jamie would try and do better, and that he loved him still very much, and would help him to recover the character he had lost, the little troubled boy was happier than he had been for a long time, and joined his brothers and sisters with a lightened heart, although unable with them to share the fond approbation which more than told them how truly and lovingly their efforts had been appreciated.

And the next day was the Sabbath—Hugh Christie's first Sabbath in England after thirteen years' absence. Oh, how different from the noisy Sabbaths spent in the midst of camp turmoil and bustle, or of long weary marches in a burning country, or of the tumult and publicity of ship-life! The chimes

from Airie church sounded out in his ears as
they had sounded in old days, only that they
seemed to speak many more things to him
than ever they had spoken before. As he
listened to their voices from a quiet walk by
the brookside where, in other years, he had
been wont to listen to them, they seemed to
chime out a " welcome home " in loud cheery
tones, and then to sink into a softer cadence,
as if to remind him of those who had bidden
him farewell long ago, but who now could
speak no greeting,—whose voices, unlike theirs,
were for ever hushed and silent. The cup of
joy is very full at many an earthly re-union;
but yet, I have known none in which there
has been infused no drop of bitterness, no
remembrance of an absent face, of a missing
welcome which, underneath all the gladness,
has its silent place deep in every heart, all
the deeper, perhaps, because it is a memory
unspoken. Only in the meeting that is to be
will there be perfect joy without shade of sorrow,
without memory of departed ones, without
yearnings for other days, without foreboding
of future separation, since then, even as the children sing, " we shall meet to part no more."

There were many kindly nods, and greetings, and congratulations as Hugh and Mary Christie, with their four children, walked once more together to the church where they had been married, and where, although it was church time, more than one inquisitive glance was directed towards the returned soldier, who had been a favourite in his boyhood in all the homes of Airie.

Perhaps there is no one circumstance which brings with it such a rush of recollection as that of finding ourselves once more in the church where, in our childhood and youth, we were accustomed to worship, and from which we may have been long separated. One reason must be that it is there that the heart's deepest chords have been touched—there, that friends have seemed nearest and dearest, and that ties, in themselves close and uniting, have seemed to be consecrated and hallowed. Hugh Christie's long years in foreign lands seemed now to him as one continuous and varied stream. He could have fancied that he had gone to sleep during one of kind old Dr. Bush's longer sermons, and having had a vision of far countries and tumultuous service,

had awakened to find a sudden transformation
of all things around him, he himself only
being the same. The venerable preacher
appeared with the comparatively youthful
form and person of Mr. Malcolm. Instead of
his mother, comfortable and respectable in her
black silk gown, with her large print Prayer-
book and sleepy voice, there sat at his side
his own wife Mary, better looking and dearer
in his eyes even than when as Mary Innes in
the next pew, she made it a sore struggle for
him to give his undivided attention to the
sermon. And where there had been no other
faces but only empty seats and unused has-
socks, he now looked with something of pride
at the four children, although Jamie, with
his Prayer-book in his hand, was busily
engaged in watching the proceedings of a
spider and a fly in a web constructed in the
furthest corner of the pew, strongly recalling
to his father's memory an occasion when he,
himself, had been similarly engaged during a
great part of the sermon when he was only
Jamie's age, and when he had been much disappointed by the sudden demolition of web,
fly, spider, and all at the hand of his father,

who looked round to discover by what means his fidgetty boy had been kept so unwontedly still during a discourse longer than usual, and concluding with a clause so specially directed against people whose eyes and thoughts wandered in church, that he could not but entertain a secret fear lest the Doctor had been observing him all the while.

Little circumstances open very frequently the flood-gates whereby a rush of recollections and associations are admitted to fill the heart and mind. So Hugh Christie, plain, matter-of-fact man as he was, found it to be, although it did not occur to him to analyze or define his feelings. A restoration of Airie church was in contemplation, and by no means too soon for its requirements; but he felt glad that it had not been begun—that the old, moth-eaten, awkwardly-shaped pew was still in its old place; that the little clumsily-cut hook which his father had contrived, and upon which had been wont to hang his mother's black silk bag, was there still; that the place where he had once torn off a piece of the baize wherewith the pew was lined was yet visible; and that the view of the singing-pew

whose glories had **early** dazzled his sight, was
still **to be obtained from** its furthest corner,
although the singers of his day had now, as
staid **matrons, and care-worn** fathers, retreated
into less conspicuous **positions,** and their sons'
**and daughters' voices sounded as theirs had
sounded in** years **gone by. Everything was
the same, and yet all was changed—all that
had life, all that the hand of Time might
sensibly affect, and Hugh Christie, in the old**
church **in which he had been baptized, and
confirmed, and married, bowed with strange
mingled feelings to return thanks for His
loving-kindness and care who changeth not.**

At the close of the **Sunday** school, which
was **held in the** afternoon, parents and children
set forth to attend an evening service which
was held fortnightly **by the clergyman of**
Airie in a little chapel **two** miles beyond the
village, and to **which came** worshippers **from
many a scattered hamlet and cottage of the
large and straggling parish, who found it difficult to attend the parish** church. **The way
led past the Carsons' cottage, and Hugh and
Maggie paused to inquire for William. He
was better, and able to sit up a little, but still**

weak. When he was strong again, he was going to leave Airie, he said, to work with an uncle at a distance, but he felt a long way from being strong now, besides being low and out of spirits. He hadn't thought to care for Ailie's going, he said, but he often wished her back now, she had come to be so much pleasanter, and had read to him now and then. However, she was better off, he knew, than ever she would have been with them, only— oh, dear! it was slow work getting well; and he supposed Hugh's father had heard everything, and wouldn't let Hugh come to see him any more. Hugh replied by a promise to come and see him whenever he could, and Maggie spoke gently and pleasantly, and hoped that he would soon get better, and then the brother and sister hastened to rejoin their parents, hearing in the distance the sound of Mrs. Carson's harsh voice as she scolded her husband for some inadvertent transgression within.

What a different atmosphere was that of the little chapel near the sailors' burying-ground before mentioned, while the distant murmur of the waves, as they washed the

beach below, mingled with the sounds of
prayer and praise which resounded with yet
more lofty harmony from the lips of those
who were gathered together for worship on
the still Sabbath evening. The short address
which followed the service found its way to
the hearts of more than one present there.
Mr. Malcolm spoke of the promise, " *Behold, I
come quickly to give unto every man according
as his work shall be;*" and of another, " *I will
come again and receive you unto myself, that
where I am there ye may be also,*" and asked
all present whether they could say of their
Saviour, "*whom having not seen we love,*"
and whether they were preparing for their
Lord. And here Hugh and Maggie exchanged
glances. The same thought had struck them
both, and that thought was carried on by the
words on Donald's grave, as with their father,
they stood by it once more, and heard from
him how he had known Ailie's father in early
life, and how little he had thought to find
his cheery welcome missing when he returned.

"Let us go home by the beach, mother,"
said Jamie; "it's not nearly sunset time yet."

" Oh yes, *do,*" echoed the others; " the tide

is not up yet, and we'll show father the place
where we made the plans."

Their parents consented, and descending
the cliff by a zig-zag path which speedily
brought them to the bottom, they pursued
their way quietly onwards, pausing every now
and then to gaze at the golden glory which
was over the waters, and to listen to the
measured fall of the light billows which,
Maggie said, seemed to sing over and over
again, "Father has come home." They all
sat down among the rocks on the spot where
the four brothers and sisters had discussed his
coming on the memorable day when they had
thought the summer would never arrive, and
Nannie was delighted at finding one or two
charred relics of their fire which had remained
above high-water mark.

"Do you remember being afraid father
wouldn't like you when he came, Maggie?" inquired Hugh, roguishly.

"And do *you* remember what you answered?" replied his sister.

"What was it?" interposed their father,
who had taken Nannie on his knee, and who
yet looked as if he could hardly realize that

15

these children were really and in truth his very own—those whom he had returned to find dearer to him than his fondest hopes had anticipated.

"Hugh said, 'he *must* love us, because we're his own children,'" replied Maggie.

"And we settled that if we were going to be cross or careless, or anything," said Nannie, "some one was to say, '*Father's coming home!*'"

"And we counted up our letters," continued Jamie; "just enough there were to last out, and Maggie read out one which said we were to be truthful, and kind, and humble, and everything else, and we were afraid we'd all seem so different from what you'd be expecting."

"Father must try and put up with you," said their mother, smiling; "I'm afraid, though, he'll begin by spoiling you all four together."

"I was thinking," replied her husband, "of the words we were hearing this evening; Maggie can say them."

"I know what you mean, father," said Maggie, repeating them slowly; "Hugh and I thought of it directly."

"What was it?" inquired Nannie.

"Maggie shall tell you," replied her father, "Maggie, can you tell Nannie what I mean?"

"Jesus is coming back," said Maggie, with an inquiring look of her blue eye, which said, "Am I right?" "Jesus is coming, and tells us to be getting ready for him."

"He says, '*I will come again and receive you unto myself*,'" continued her father; "dear children, are we getting ready for him?"

"Do we always know how?" asked Nannie. "I wish Jesus would come here and tell us exactly what to do, and then we'd be sure to be right."

"What made you each wish to be doing something for father, Nannie?" inquired her mother, "why were you all thinking of what would please him?"

"Because we loved him," replied Nannie, quickly, "we loved him although we hadn't any of us seen him to remember."

"And we knew he loved us," interposed Jamie.

"How could you know that, Jamie, when I hadn't been with you?" inquired his father, the elder ones saw, with a view towards eliciting the reply which was on his lips,—

"Why, every one told us about you—mother and all the people that knew you, and then you wrote so much love to us, and sent us things, and, even when—when—I had—" Jamie became confused and troubled in voice, "even then, mother said she knew you'd love me still."

"There is a verse," continued his father, "which speaks of One who will soon come again to receive the account of what we have done for him, which says, '*Whom having not seen, we love?*'"

"'*And in whom believing we rejoice,*' continued Maggie, "like we rejoiced when we thought of your coming, father."

"And we know how he loved us, and gave himself for us," pursued her father. "Our poor earthly love is a very small thing compared with his, who died for us. Nannie says she wishes that she could hear Jesus say what he would have her do for him before he comes. How did you know what I would have you do?"

"Your letters told us," replied Hugh; "even if mother hadn't told us, we'd have known."

His father smiled at Nannie, as he touched the Testament—her prize Testament—which she held in her hand.

"I know," exclaimed Jamie; "the Bible has God's letters to us. We should read it to know what he wishes us to do."

"He has said, 'If ye love me, keep my commandments,'" replied his father, "and 'his commandments are not grievous." My children, I thank you over and over again, for your love to me, and, I have thought, ever since I came, of the lesson it may be to us all. All of us have something to do for Jesus; he says he has left to 'every man his work.' And he tells us, 'Be ye also ready.' He sends his Spirit to shed abroad love in our hearts which inclines us to serve him, and his word to tell us what to do. The time given us is very short to show our gratitude to him who has done so much for us.

"It used to make us so careful, when we said, 'Father's coming home,' said Maggie, musingly, "but I think it ought to make us much more, if we always thought *Jesus* is coming."

"Let us all try to be thinking of it more,"

said her father, "your own plans will teach you. Maggie tried to show her love by denying herself in work for others. '*Inasmuch as ye did it unto the least of these my brethren, ye did it unto me*' will be our Lord's word to those who have for his sake lived for the poor and needy whom he calls his brethren. And Hugh has learnt that '*he that humbleth himself shall be exalted,*' and so, if we are good soldiers, we shall be willing to bear the cross here, for Christ's sake."

"And Jamie learnt that his father would love him still, although he had been wrong," interposed his mother, " when he was sad and sorry for it all ; just as our Father when he comes to take the kingdom, will never refuse to own any one of his children who mourns for sins, and seeks pardon for his Son's sake."

"And, father," said the little one, as she nestled into the place which she had already found to be her own ; "say something for me too."

" Nannie has taught us that when we are really seeking to make ready for our Lord's coming, we shall always be guided into doing

what he would have us do, just as she
knew exactly the best plan to choose."

"Only Hugh and Maggie helped me," whispered Nannie, with a pleased face; "they
thought you'd like it, father."

The sun was setting over the sea, and it
was time to go home, but still they all lingered,
—even the children seeming to enter into the
tranquil enjoyment of the scene.

"God has been very good to us," said their
father, "it seems as if we couldn't praise him
enough, but we can all remember to try and
show our thanks by getting ready for him as
well as we can, while we have time. Our
chaplain out in India used to say that even if
we die, our work for God doesn't die."

"Let the children each give us a text to
remember it by," rejoined his wife, "a little
bit of God's word seems like a peg for hang-
ing on all the talking and thinking there's
been about it."

So Hugh began,—

"*Behold, I come quickly; and my reward
is with me to give every man according as his
work shall be.*"

And Maggie said,—

"*If I go and prepare a place for you, I will come again and receive you unto myself; that where I am, there ye may be also.*"

Jamie could not think of one at first, but his mother helped him, and he read out,—

"*For the Son of man is as a man taking a far journey, who left his house, and gave authority to his servants, and to every man his work, and commanded the porter to watch.*"

"*Watch ye therefore: for ye know not when the master of the house cometh, at even, or at midnight, or at cock-crowing, or in the morning; lest coming suddenly he find you sleeping.*"

And little Nannie, who had been peeping here and there through the pages of her Testament, and, having placed her finger on one particular text, waited inquiringly to know whether it would do, read slowly and carefully, the words which, however, she already knew by heart,—

Surely I come quickly. Amen. Even so, come, Lord Jesus.